D0640002

"Where do you think we've met before?"

Lauren couldn't answer. It was the last thing she'd expected Joel Rockwell to say. She closed her eyes, smelled the fragrance of orange blossom, felt a soft warm breeze touch her skin. The veranda was in darkness. The deep resonant voice probed again.

"Where? Do you remember where?"

"Spain." She was terrified by the sense of unreality that surrounded her. Finally she looked up at him. His gaze was fixed on her intently. *Please,* she thought, *don't stare at me like that. We're not strangers.*

Silence. "Are you sure?" he asked at last.

She nodded. "Yes. I'm sure."

There was a slight pause. "I've never been in Spain," he said.

Books by Karen Van Der Zee

HARLEQUIN ROMANCES

HARLEQUIN PRESENTS

These books may be available at your local bookseller.

For a list of all titles currently available, send your name and address to:

Harlequin Reader Service
P.O. Box 52040, Phoenix, AZ 85072-2040
Canadian address: P.O. Box 2800, Postal Station A,
5170 Yonge St., Willowdale, Ont. M2N 5T5

Soul
Ties

Karen van der Zee

Harlequin Books

TORONTO • NEW YORK • LONDON
AMSTERDAM • PARIS • SYDNEY • HAMBURG
STOCKHOLM • ATHENS • TOKYO • MILAN

Original hardcover edition published in 1984
by Mills & Boon Limited

ISBN 0-373-02652-8

Harlequin Romance first edition October 1984

Copyright © 1984 by Karen Van Der Zee.
Philippine copyright 1984. Australian copyright 1984.
Cover illustration copyright © 1984 by Will Davies.
All rights reserved. Except for use in any review, the reproduction or utilization
of this work in whole or in part in any form by any electronic, mechanical
or other means, now known or hereafter invented, including xerography,
photocopying and recording, or in any information storage or retrieval system,
is forbidden without the permission of the publisher, Harlequin Enterprises
Limited, 225 Duncan Mill Road, Don Mills, Ontario, Canada M3B 3K9. All the
characters in this book have no existence outside the imagination of the
author and have no relation whatsoever to anyone bearing the same name
or names. They are not even distantly inspired by any individual known
or unknown to the author, and all the incidents are pure invention.

The Harlequin trademarks, consisting of the words HARLEQUIN ROMANCE
and the portrayal of a Harlequin, are trademarks of Harlequin Enterprises
Limited; the portrayal of a Harlequin is registered in the United States Patent
and Trademark Office and in the Canada Trade Marks Office.

Printed in U.S.A.

CHAPTER ONE

'HAVEN'T we met somewhere before?'

Mortified, Lauren heard the worn-out line slip out of her mouth. It hung in the air like a profanity, damning and irredeemable. Couldn't she have thought of something a little more original?

The tall, dark man to whom she had directed the question regarded her coolly. From the look in the steely grey eyes it was clear that he wasn't charmed in the least.

If somebody gave me that line, I wouldn't be either, she couldn't help thinking, remembering the clumsy advances of various clumsy men. Although her question had not been meant as a come-on, not a soul on the entire island of Java would believe it, and certainly not this obviously sophisticated American. He'd seen and heard it all before. Nothing impressed him, least of all her and her tacky opening gambit.

She *knew* this man. Lauren was very sure of that, although she could not at all remember when and where she'd seen him before. She had no clear recollection of having met him. All during this endless, boring meeting in the stifling office, she'd been acutely aware of him, sensing a connection she didn't understand. His lean body and darkly tanned face were not actually familiar to her, but there was something about him, something that went deeper then mere physical appearance, that set off in her a deep sense of recognition. It made her unaccountably nervous and not a little bit excited. Her rational mind might be confused, but her instincts were not. *She knew this man!*

'I don't believe so.' His expression was not encouraging.

5

He thinks I'm trying to pick him up, she thought, suddenly aware of her wrinkled dress and the shine on her face. Her hair was escaping from the knot on top of her head and she tucked it behind her ears, uncomfortably aware of her dishevelled appearance. It wasn't easy to look fresh and immaculate in the tropics, and certainly not when you'd been driving in an open Toyota Land Cruiser for two hours and then spent two more hours in a stuffy little office without air-conditioning.

Bravely she lifted her chin and stared right back at him. 'I know you,' she said stubbornly.

'Well,' he countered with maddening calm, '*I* don't know *you*.'

Obviously there was nothing more to be said. She certainly wasn't going to begin an argument over it. All that remained to be done was for her to get out of this conversation with her pride intact.

Lauren, my girl, she said to herself, give it your all!

She raised herself to her full five foot eight inches, squared her shoulders and smiled her best smile. 'Maybe it was someone who looked like you,' she suggested, knowing that whatever it was that she recognised had nothing to do with his looks. 'Now that I think of it, I remember him being polite, friendly and charming,' she improvised. Her meaning, that he was none of these things, was clear. She turned and swung out of the room with as much dignity as she could muster.

The meeting had broken up, but some people were still standing around, talking. Most of them Lauren had never seen before. It wasn't a meeting she would have ordinarily attended, but Ed, her boss, had needed to go to Jakarta at the last minute and had sent her to take his place. It had been truly exhausting. Despite the fact that she had been taking daily language lessons for months now and could manage quite well around the house and in the market, a business meeting in Indonesian was still a taxing affair.

Emerging in the steaming heat of mid-afternoon, she blinked against the fierce sunlight. Fishing her sunglasses from her bag, she swapped them for her regular ones and searched for the keys to her Toyota. Having found them, she unlocked the door, crawled behind the wheel and put the keys into the ignition. A face appeared at the window and her heart gave a curious little leap. The man looked at her, dark brows raised in question.

'No driver?' he asked, grey eyes cool.

Was it any of his business? Lauren gave him a long, silent look. 'My driver is sick,' she said at last. 'High fever. It seems to be going around. It's the mango season, they tell me.' Everybody blamed everything on the blooming mango trees.

'Ah, yes, the mango season.'

Turning the key, she made the engine roar. He stepped away from the vehicle and Lauren rolled out into the dusty street without another word or look. Ahead lay a two-hour drive back to Semarang. She longed for a cold shower and a cold drink. She even longed for her bed with the lumpy kapok mattress.

She couldn't get the man out of her thoughts.

She was angry. Her hands were tight on the steering wheel, her jaws clenched hard. She felt humiliated by the man's words, his manner, the way he had looked at her as if she were some two-bit tramp out for a good time. And she was furious with herself for her ill-chosen opening gambit. *Haven't we met somewhere before?* She groaned inwardly. Was it any wonder he had reacted the way he had?

Who was this man?

When she had first seen him at the meeting, she had felt her senses thrill. It had been instantaneous, like an electric shock setting off sparks all through her body

Across the room their eyes had met, locked for a magical moment, and between them something had flared, something intangible but very real.

Love at first sight?

She'd heard about it, read about it. Was that what it was? If so, it seemed to be a one-sided experience, considering the man's cool, disdainful behaviour towards her. Had she imagined the current leaping up between them?

Lauren sighed and concentrated on the dry, rutted road ahead of her. The Javanese countryside is beautiful, and despite her fatigue she couldn't help enjoying the drive. So many shades of green! In the distance blue-green hills sloped softly against a bright blue sky. Terraced rice paddies formed an artful design, decorating the landscape with graceful line and colour. Some paddies were flooded and ready for planting, some were emerald green with young rice plants, others a yellowish green, ready for harvesting.

The road led past many villages, clusters of small houses with red-tiled roofs sitting amid coconut groves, clumps of bamboo and banana plants. Children played in the dust, being kept company by chickens, ducks, goats and dogs.

It was almost six when Lauren reached the outskirts of Semarang and the light was fading fast. The traffic was heavy and it took all her attention to manoeuvre through it without being wiped off the face of the earth by an inter-city bus passing traffic on the wrong side of the road. A motorcycle carrying a family of five swerved past her at dizzying speed. A minute later she barely avoided running into a cyclist who came dashing out of an alley with several dozen live chickens dangling by their feet from his handlebars. Her heart in her throat, she uttered something unprintable, surprising herself. Generally speaking she was a mild-mannered person.

People truly thought they were immortal in this place! Three months in Indonesia and she still wasn't used to the horrors of the traffic.

From the big mosque the muezzin began his chanting, calling people to worship. The sounds of his amplified voice reverberated over the town with an odd metallic whine. It was fully dark now. Kerosene lamps lighted foodstalls everywhere along the roadside. Canvas shades that kept the sun out during the day advertised the menus—*Nasi Ramas*, *Ayam Goreng*, *Bakmie*, *Sate Sapi*. The spicy smells drifted on the warm evening air and Lauren's stomach growled inelegantly. She was ravenous!

She arrived home, parked the Toyota in the garage and went inside. From the kitchen the aroma of cooking food wafted towards her. But first a shower. No, first something to drink. She drank two glasses of water standing right next to the refrigerator, while Yanti, her cook/cleaner, watched and giggled. She was a thin little thing, less than five foot tall, making Lauren feel like the Jolly Green Giant. Actually, in Indonesia, most people made her feel like that.

Dashing into her bedroom, she stripped off her clothes and dived into the shower. The cool water refreshed her. She shampooed her hair and rolled it up in a towel, then wrapping a sarong around her, she went into the dining room and was given *nasi goreng*—fried rice and onions, shrimp, pieces of chicken, spices and a fried egg. She loved Indonesian food, and having given Yanti free rein in the kitchen, she ate like a queen.

After dinner she took her coffee to her bedroom and lay down, air-conditioner on. It was seven o'clock. She was wiped out and all she wanted to do was read for a while and go to sleep.

She couldn't sleep.

She couldn't read.

She kept thinking about the grey-eyed man. In her

mind she saw him again, making his presentation, speaking fluent Indonesian. He radiated calm, self-confidence, authority. His very presence commanded respect. Cool and self-possessed, he looked like someone who wouldn't lose his composure at the sight of a volcanic eruption.

Who was he? Where had she seen him before? When? Not recently, at any rate. Maybe it had been years ago, when she was a child. Her thoughts struggled back through the years. She'd lived in many places. Her father was an officer in the U.S. Navy and her family had moved around the globe from one base to another like a small band of gypsies. She'd met many people— too many. Like a circus parade they'd marched through her life and she couldn't possibly remember all those faces. Maybe he'd been one of those anonymous faces she'd once glimpsed at a party.

Probably, her rational mind said.

No, her intuition said. There was something very special about this man; her reaction had been too strong for just a casual recognition. She had the most disconcerting feeling that she knew him *well*. But if this was so, why then couldn't she remember anything?

Lauren sighed with frustration and watched a small pinkish-grey lizard scoot across the ceiling. Indifferently she glanced around the room. It was depressingly bare, like the rest of the house, containing only the necessary furniture and not much more. She felt bare herself, empty, frayed around the edges.

She was lonely, a strange, timeless longing for something she didn't even understand, something that came from the deepest core of her being. For the longest time—an endless time, it seemed—she had had a sense of waiting, yet not knowing what it was she was waiting for.

So far her life had lacked nothing. She had had a happy childhood, loving parents, a brother, a sister, clothes and food and security of every kind. Still, ever since she was a child she had had the feeling something was missing—something essential. There was a secret part of her that felt empty and incomplete. Of course, when she had been a child, it had only been an undefined feeling she had been incapable of expressing in words. Still, it had always been very real.

Sometimes when she sat by the sea, alone, listening to the timeless sound of endless waves washing ashore, she would be gripped by an uncontrollable melancholy, as if somewhere beyond the distant horizon something or someone was calling out to her and she could not come and she could not answer.

The same bewildering feeling would take hold of her when she played her favourite piece of music on the piano. It was called *Memories* and she could play it by heart. She would play, almost in a trance, with tears streaming down her cheeks. No other music, no matter how beautiful or emotional, had this effect on her.

Lauren hadn't played the piano for a long time now; a piano didn't fit her lifestyle. After she had graduated from college she had worked in the States for a couple of years, then became restless. She went overseas again, leading a shifting, drifting life, moving from one short-term contract to another, living in hotels for weeks on end or in temporary housing using other people's furniture. Her present job was the first long-term contract she had managed to get: one year on Java, Indonesia, designing and conducting training programmes for village women working in small industries.

No piano in her luggage. I should have learned to play the guitar, she thought. At least that I could have carried around with me. For the music in her life she had to resort to tapes and a small stereo.

She had few material possessions, but to make up for that she owned an extensive wardrobe, an eclectic collection of garments and accessories she had acquired over the years in various places—a blue and gold silk sari, a jade green kimono, hand-knitted sweaters from Iceland (now in mothball storage in the apartment of a friend in Bethesda, Maryland), long tie-dye skirts, harem pants, cotton kaftans, brightly coloured shawls. She had a collection of hair combs, jewellery of silver and turquoise and jade and African glass beads. Following fashion was a bore—she bought what she liked and wore it for many years, mixing and matching as the spirit moved her.

Sleep was not forthcoming. She shouldn't have had that coffee.

Twenty minutes and many sighs later she got up, draped herself in a batik wrap-around dress and began to brush her still-damp hair. There was no need for her to lie in bed and go quietly crazy on a Friday night. She could go to the Candi Baru Pub, have a drink and play darts.

Playing darts was not her forte, but fortunately the players who gathered on Friday nights weren't great fanatics about the game, not even the British ones. They showed goodhumoured tolerance for her brave attempts. After all, one could not expect too much expertise at darts from an American female.

A game was in full progress when she entered the bar and a good time was being held by all. She perched on an empty stool next to Sten, who put a possessive arm around her.

'Lauren, my love, I was waiting for you. What can I get you?'

'Peace of mind,' she said.

'On ice?'

She nodded.

'Campari and soda,' Sten said to the bartender, rather superfluously since the man was already busy pouring. He was familiar with Lauren's wishes.

Sten grimaced at her. 'I don't understand how you can drink that stuff. It tastes vile, like medicine.'

'I'm a sick person.'

'No, you're not. Sexy, not sick.'

'Shut up, Sten!'

Sten was from Denmark, short, dark, with brown eyes, which goes to prove you can't count on anything any more.

'Have you decided yet?' he whispered seductively, leaning closer. Apparently the semi-dark of the bar made him amorous and brave. The area was illuminated by only two rattan lamps with low-watt bulbs.

'Decided what?'

'When you're going to take me up on my offer.'

Lauren drank her Campari. 'What offer?'

'A night of ecstasy and passion. Just you and me and a bottle of wine.'

'Oh, that.'

He looked wounded. 'Well, have you decided when?'

'As a matter of fact, I have.' She smiled winningly.

'You have? When?'

'August the fifteenth, ten o'clock, your place.'

His face collapsed. 'You're not nice, Lauren.'

'Neither are you.' August the fifteenth was the day his wife was returning from Denmark. 'You should be grateful,' she said soothingly. 'I'm saving you from sin and damnation, not to mention divorce.'

'Who wants to be saved?' he moaned, staring gloomily into his beer. 'I'm lonely, don't you know that? I've been dreaming of a tall, blue-eyed brunette in my arms.'

'Keep dreaming,' she said, stone-hearted. His wife was a petite blonde, sweet and pretty.

In the corner behind the bar the television was on, showing traditional Javanese dancing. Sipping her drink, Lauren watched the sinuous bodies in brightly coloured costumes undulating slowly across the screen. The sound had been turned off. Instead the radio, from some hidden place, was gushing forth sentimental love songs in English. The combination was fascinating. Not every day do you see Javanese girls swaying sensuously to Engelbert Humperdinck's *Please Release Me, Let Me Go*.

She had finished her drink, pushed the glass aside and reached for the dish of peanuts.

Her heart stopped—well, almost.

She was looking straight into the cool grey eyes of the Mystery Man. He was sitting at the other end of the curved bar and he was watching her. She hadn't noticed him coming in.

Her hand shook and the peanuts rolled from her nerveless fingers across the bar top. Sten began to gather them, giving her a searching look.

'What's the matter with you?' he asked, surprised. 'You look as white as a sheet. Let me get you another drink.'

Lauren felt hot and cold at the same time. 'Nothing. My wrist gave out, that's all.' She rubbed it demonstratively.

'Dengue fever,' Sten diagnosed cheerfully. 'You may think you're dying, but you'll feel better in five days.' He felt her forehead. 'You're hot.'

She slapped his hand away. Her hand still shaking, she picked up her fresh Campari and took a long drink. Her heart was racing. She was aware of the man's eyes—burning holes straight through her.

'Who's that guy over there?' asked Sten. 'I've never seen him before.'

'I don't know.' It was the truth. She didn't even know his name. Yes, she did. *Rockwell*. She'd heard it mentioned at the meeting that afternoon.

'Oh, come on! You can record the vibrations on a tape!'

He was probably right. The vibrations, or whatever the man was sending out, were zeroing in on her nervous system. She managed to bring the glass back to her mouth and gulped down half the contents. It didn't do her any good. She needed something a lot stronger

than watered-down Campari. She stared blindly down
into the peanut dish, not daring to move her eyes.

'Lauren! Are you playing?'

The game had finished and new teams were being
made up. Relief flooded her. She felt as if someone had
rescued her from Purgatory and she slid off her stool,
calling out an affirmative answer in a throaty voice that
didn't sound at all like her own.

Her eyes flicked over the names on the board. She
knew them all, except for one.

Joel.

The Mystery Man. Joel Rockwell.

He was on the other team, his turn right after hers.
Why had she expected him to stay put at the bar?

When her turn came she could feel him standing
behind her as she positioned herself for the throw. Her
body grew tense. Her arm and wrist moved awkwardly
and her aim was nothing short of abominable. Two out
of the three darts didn't even hit the board.

'Have another drink, love,' suggested someone.

Feeling like a fool, Lauren stepped aside without a
word. Joel Rockwell moved forward, aimed and hit a
double twenty. His movements were smooth and
controlled and she watched him as he threw his second
dart. A single twenty. Everyone whooped for joy.

He wore teal blue slacks and a white sports shirt. His
arms were tanned and covered with dark hair. A gold
watch with a wide leather band encircled his wrist.
Muscles tightened and relaxed in a quick, fluid
movement, and the third dart hit a single eighteen. He
was a superb marksman, that much was obvious. He'd
been a superb speaker that afternoon, too, speaking
fluent Indonesian, rolling his r's like a native.

His turn over, he stepped aside and came towards
her, eyes sliding over her in quick appraisal.

'You made it back,' he stated.

'So I did,' she returned coolly. She was glad she

looked more presentable now than she had that
afternoon. With an effort she tried to relax her body,
but her muscles felt rigid like wrought iron. Her heart
was hammering against her ribs and she felt ridiculously
nervous. Why did this man have such a strong effect on
her? Why did she have the feeling that behind that cool
exterior somebody else was hiding, somebody she
knew? Looking away, she noticed Sten coming towards
her with her glass from the bar. He handed it to her,
then looked at Joel.

'Played darts before, I take it?'

After the introductions, the two of them began a
conversation and Lauren slipped away gratefully,
watching the other players and waiting for her turn.

She didn't do much better the second time around.
Sten took her wrist and examined it. 'Something wrong
with this after all?' he asked, and she jerked her hand
from his grip, catching Joel's eyes as they swept over
her.

Conversation flowed around her, only fragments of it
reaching her brain. '. . . *wife scraping open the skin on
his back . . . smelly ointment . . . supposed to cure
headache . . . I gave. . . .*' Her thoughts were on Joel and
she watched him surreptitiously.

'Your turn.' Sten handed her his darts and she moved
into position.

'Aim for the board,' Sten suggested, and she glared at
him.

The game went on, but she was hardly conscious of
it, throwing the darts automatically. Joel did not speak
to her again, didn't even look in her direction. She
heard him talking about building boats, caught only a
word here and there but didn't grasp the meaning.

When the game was over, Sten stepped in front of
her, lifted her glasses off her nose and peered through
them, then replaced them. 'Are you sure,' he said, 'that
you don't need new lenses?'

She couldn't even think of an answer. She stared at him numbly, then turned and hurried out of the place without a word of goodbye to anyone. She couldn't believe herself. She was acting like she had never acted before.

She hadn't even put the key in the door of the Toyota yet when Joel Rockwell appeared by her side. He had a key in his hand too, as if on his way home as well.

'Is something wrong?' he asked evenly.

'I don't know what you mean.'

'You were acting very strangely.'

'What makes you think that? You don't know me. Maybe it's the way I am.' She didn't look at him. Her heart was about to jump out of her chest.

'Did I make you nervous?'

She gave a short, shaky laugh, not answering.

'Do you still think you know me?'

Lauren looked up, seeing stars in patches of dark sky visible through shadowy palm-fronds. Did she? Oh, yes, she did! She knew him. She sensed it with a certainty beyond any logic or reason. And what was worse, she was attracted to him. Every cell of her body was aware of his presence. She had never felt such a strong sense of connection with any man.

She felt suddenly terribly frightened. There was something mysterious and unreal about all this. The sultry, torrid night air made it hard to breathe. She was aware of a vibrating tension between them.

'Do you?' he persisted. 'Do you still think you know me?'

For a moment she hesitated. 'Do you still think *you* don't know *me*?'

There was an almost imperceptible pause. 'I've never met you,' he said. 'I would have remembered.'

He could mean more than one thing with that, but Lauren didn't ask. She was silent, noticing the small night sounds all around them, the buzzing of insects, the *toke*, *toke* of a gecko.

'You didn't answer my question,' said Joel Rockwell, his voice quiet in the dark.

She swallowed nervously. 'I know you,' she said.

Somehow she managed to open the car door, get in and drive away.

Lauren woke up at five and could no longer sleep. She went to the kitchen and made a pot of tea, taking it back to the verandah off her bedroom. Every morning before getting ready for the day she sat there with her tea, a peaceful ritual she enjoyed.

At five it was only barely light. Through the morning mist the sun seemed only a hazy orange ball suspended in the sky. The air was filled with the noises of roosters and birds, giving the illusion of being in the country. From a nearby mosque the muezzin began his chanting, his voice sounding sleepy and lazy and almost feminine.

Drinking her tea, Lauren surveyed the view. Her house was built on a hill and overlooked a *kampong* below where small houses with red-tiled roofs huddled closely together. A young man with a thick mop of dark hair, wearing shorts and sleeveless shirt, crossed a dusty courtyard carrying a blue plastic bucket. A scrawny dog followed him. Pigeons cooed from the roof of his house.

Something white and fluffy floated through the air, then another one and another one. Cotton balls? Snowflakes? More and more were carried past her on the morning breeze. Searching, she noticed a tree from which they were coming. At the base if its trunk the ground was white as if covered by snow. A kapok tree shedding its seeds. Fascinated, Lauren watched the fluffy balls floating through the air.

She poured more tea. The sun was growing brighter now and more and more people were emerging from their houses. The muezzin was silent, and suddenly bells began to ring from the chapel of the mission hospital nearby.

She wished she could drink in the peace of this morning and make it her own. But the shadow of the previous day still hung in her mind, clouding her thoughts.

At six she got up and went inside to take a shower. It was Saturday. Working in a government office she was expected to keep government hours, which meant working on Saturday mornings.

Ed had returned from Jakarta and she gave him her report on the meeting she had attended on his behalf. They shared an office, a big, rather shabby room with old wooden desks and glaring fluorescent light.

Ed, pear-shaped and balding, was a chain-smoker, filling the office with the spicy aroma of Kretek cigarettes. He was in his fifties and single, pretending to be thirty and virile. He combed the few hairs he had carefully across the empty patch of skull on the top of his head.

Before the morning was over Lauren was involved in a violent argument with him about the role of women in Indonesian society. His notions about women in general were appalling. The dungeons of his mind had seen no fresh air since the Dark Ages, and it made it extremely difficult to work for him. How he had ever ended up working in a female-orientated programme such as this one would for ever be a mystery to her.

Ed needed desperately to have his consciousness raised, providing he had one, which she doubted at times. One evening with her friend Barbara in Bethesda would do him a world of good. Too bad Lauren wasn't more of a fanatic herself, or she'd give it a try herself. But she had never been a pursuer of Great Causes, although her loyalties were clearly defined.

Needless to say she was relieved when the morning was over and she could go home.

It was quite by coincidence that Lauren overheard a conversation that afternoon. She was in Galael's supermarket (a minuscule imitation of the Western variety) checking out the selection of jams when she heard Anne Furgeson's voice in the next aisle. She was informing some other (to Lauren) invisible person of the arrival of a New Man in town, a real hunk of masculinity by the name of Joel Rockwell.

With her eyes fastened hypnotically on a jar of blackberry jam from Holland, Lauren listened, collecting facts and information.

Joel was a tropical marine biologist (she'd guessed something of that nature) employed by International Fisheries. He had been transferred from Surabaya where he had spent the last six months. Before that he had lived in the States for a while and earlier on he had spent several years in various places in the East. He was good-looking, said Anne, tall, interesting, sexy. She'd trade her husband in for him at a moment's notice.

Lauren heartily disliked Anne Furgeson. She was always cutting down her husband in one way or another, behind his back or right in front of him. It seemed to Lauren the ultimate infidelity. Anne was pretty in an artificial sort of way. Smooth and silken, she was always made up to perfection as if perpetually en route to a party. She looked as if she wore make-up to bed, just in case. Lauren didn't trust her. There were some jagged bits and pieces craftily camouflaged by that glossy polish of her appearance.

Joel Rockwell had moved into the McKinney house, said Anne.

Lauren reached for the nearest jar of preserves and moved out of the aisle and away from the reaches of Anne's voice.

It can't be true! she thought wildly, dumping a bag of sugar in the cart. *Not the McKinney house!*

She grabbed a bottle of corn oil off the shelf and

walked on automatically, taking breakfast cereal, a box of tissues and bread and depositing them in the cart. *It can't be true*, she kept thinking. *It can't be true!*

The McKinney house was right next to hers. Of all the houses in Semarang, why that one?

Because it was leased by International Fisheries and they'd had their employees in it for years. Simple.

She drove home, passing the McKinney house on the way. It was set back from the road a little and palms, bamboo and flowering bushes hid most of it from view. It was a beautiful old Dutch colonial house with large rooms and high ceilings and big verandahs. She'd been inside it when the McKinneys had still been living there a few weeks ago and she knew that it was a big, rambling house—much too big, it would seem, for a single man.

Who said he was single? He could have a wife and six children for all she knew. But no, Anne would have mentioned it; she was sure of that. Anne spouted her knowledge like a geyser, leaving nothing out. Lauren knew the lady well enough by now.

It was three o'clock when she came back. Leaving Yanti to take care of the groceries, Lauren took a glass of water and a banana and retreated to the cool of her bedroom, where she lay down on the bed with a book.

She fell asleep.

She was out cold till five. Still groggy, she swept the hair out of her face and made her way to the kitchen, barefoot, and tying a sarong around her as she went. Coffee, she needed coffee, three cups at least. She made a pot, Java-style, scooping powdery grounds straight into the grey-blue enamel pot (bought in the *pasar* downtown) and filling it up with boiling water. It made a very robust cup of coffee, beating instant every time, in her opinion, and you didn't even have to sail the high seas for it to taste good.

As she was drinking her *kopi tubruk*, sitting on her

living room verandah where orchids in hanging baskets bloomed lavishly, she remembered the invitation. Dinner at the Stewards' at seven-thirty. She felt a sudden odd premonition.

Joel would be at the party.

She had no idea why she knew, but she knew. A nervous excitement took hold of her. She considered staying at home and telling Josie she was suffering from some mysterious tropical virus, but she knew she would not. She would go to the dinner; she wanted to see Joel again.

She couldn't believe herself.

Common sense told her to stay away from him, but all her other instincts clamoured to be with him. She took a deep breath. Tonight she would not make a fool of herself. Tonight she was going to be perfectly cool and composed.

She took her time getting ready, choosing a long silk dress she'd bought in Singapore with a long slit on one side. It had the most gorgeous shades of violet, blue, lavender and turquoise, and it fitted her to perfection. She draped her hair on top of her head and put on long silver earrings.

She drove to the Stewards' house, half an hour late. She made her grand entrance, her eyes sweeping casually around the room, surveying the guests.

Joel Rockwell was not there.

Lauren had spent two hours decorating herself and she felt a disappointment so acute, she wondered if she were losing her sanity.

Josie, her hostess, looked her over with undisguised envy. 'You look positively stunning,' she said.

So she should. Two hours of bathing, shampooing, creaming, buffing, polishing and brushing was not nothing.

'Thank you,' she said modestly.

'You're the only one I know,' Josie added, 'who looks sexy wearing glasses.'

That was a good thing, too, because the frames had cost her a small fortune. Contact lenses were not for her. For some reason unknown to science her eyes didn't like their intrusion. For a while she had tried, but it had been nothing but a nuisance, and when finally she had actually lost one of the wretched things in a hayfield (her grandfather owned a farm in Iowa) she'd said the hell with it, forget it, it's not worth the agony.

She smiled at Josie. Josie was one of those people who have a generous soul, a heart of gold, a talent for gourmet cooking, but no idea whatsoever about how to apply lipstick. She looked plain and colourless, but her smile was sweet and everybody loved her as much as they loved her cooking, maybe even more. Josie, soft and round and loving, had no sharp edges, no sharp tongue.

The house was filled with the most delectable aromas. At the bar, Josie's red-haired, freckled husband, Steve, poured her a Campari and soda. Having exchanged a few pleasantries with him, Lauren took her glass outside where several people had settled themselves on the large, covered verandah. Rattan lamps spread an intimate light and potted plants were grouped around artfully. She lowered herself into a rattan chair, returning greetings, and listened absently to a disjointed conversation that moved from local politics to salt manufacturing to the delights of a lazy week on the island of Bali.

For some reason she was terribly restless. She kept swinging her legs, tapping her fingers on the chair, twirling her glass, and fiddling with her earrings. Would Joel Rockwell still come? If so, she'd better shape up. If she was so nervous while he wasn't even here, how was she going to be cool and composed when he arrived? She got up and walked into the yard, over the yellowed grass, to the edge, where a cement wall marked the end. Leaning against it, she looked out over the *kampong*

below where low-watt bulbs lighted the small houses.
Way beyond was the Java Sea, and she could see some
of the lighted ships anchored just offshore. There was a
half moon, and a multitude of stars sparkled in the sky.

How long she stood there, gazing out over the
kampong, she didn't know, but suddenly she felt a
strange prickling sensation going down her spine. Her
breath caught in her throat. She knew that if she turned
around, she would find Joel Rockwell standing there.
Slowly she turned.

He was there, silhouetted against the vast expanse of
the lighted living room window. His face was in
shadow.

'*Selamat malam*,' he said smoothly.

'Hi,' she said shakily.

'Josie sent me to tell you that dinner is being served.'

'Thank you.' Quickly she walked across the grass and
past him into the house, catching the faint fragrance of
his aftershave as she went by.

Joel had been seated straight across from her. Eyes
cast down, she concentrated on her shrimp cocktail,
gathering courage. She racked her brains for something
to say, something brilliant, witty, or maybe just funny.
The shrimp cocktail was superb. Her mind was a blank.
She never had trouble talking to men. She wasn't in the
least a shy, insecure wallflower, so what was the matter
with her?

She ate in silence, not joining in the conversation.
Across the table Joel Rockwell was talking with interest
and animation, but he never said a word to her. Lauren
wondered if it was by design or just coincidence.

'You two haven't been neighbours for a week yet,'
Steve commented, 'you're not fighting already, are
you?'

Lauren looked up.

Joel looked up.

'Neighbours?' he asked, looking at her with a frown.

'You didn't *know*?' squealed Josie.

He shook his head slowly, eyes still on Lauren's face.

She swallowed. 'I only found out today. I heard Anne Furgeson talk about it in Galael's.' She didn't like the way Joel was observing her. It wasn't her fault he lived next to her. She'd had nothing to do with it. So why was she feeling so defensive?

Conversation resumed and the next course was brought in. Except for an occasional polite question, Joel did not speak to her. She tried to ignore him, but it was impossible. Every time she looked up he was sitting there across from her radiating charm all over the room except to her. A few times his eyes skimmed over her, uninterested, and slowly a strong resentment began to build up inside her. *He* was ignoring *her*! The miserable, arrogant, insufferable. . . . She couldn't think of a word strong enough. She felt humiliated to the core.

She hated him!

She felt a deep, aching sadness. She wanted to cry.

They kept meeting, unplanned and by coincidence, in all kinds of places. Joel would greet her politely, then ignore her. Lauren felt her anger growing; her desperation too. Every time she saw him her heart made somersaults. In spite of her anger she felt an increasing attraction to him. She invented a hundred reasons and excuses to go to his house (leaky taps, broken iron, telephone out of order, could she borrow a book? A cup of flour? His pyjamas?) but her pride prevented her from going.

Her appetite disappeared and her sleep was restless and full of dreams of Joel. He had invaded every part of her life. She began to feel tired and irritable, and her work suffered.

She thought about him all the time.

Tomorrow when I wake up, she kept thinking, I'll remember who he is. The knowledge was there, somewhere in her memory, and sooner or later it would come to her. Her subconscious would relinquish its secret and in a blinding flash of insight all would be clear.

It didn't happen. Not for two weeks. Every time she saw him she would feel the tingle of recognition, the sense of familiarity, but his identity remained a mystery.

Why did they keep meeting? It was beginning to look like a conspiracy. Something strange was happening—too many coincidences, like a bad novel. It was as if an invisible web was being spun around them, drawing them irrevocably together.

Still, every time they met, he treated her with cool indifference. Lauren became more and more convinced that his cool appearance was a lie. The tension between them was so thick it was impossible for him to be untouched by it. She was shaken by it every time. Her anger flourished like a weed. How dared he treat her in such a way? Ignore her? Ignore the sparks flying between them? The crackling electricity? And why? *Why?*

Lauren was tempted to go up to him, shout at him, anything to get his attention, anything but that cool regard, the slight lifting of his mouth, the disdainful raising of an eyebrow.

There had to be a reason for his behaviour. She searched her mind, coming up with nothing except that initial encounter weeks ago when she had asked him if they hadn't met before. Surely it couldn't be that? He wouldn't just blatantly ignore her simply because of one stupid question.

They met again at a party and like always exchanged polite greetings—Joel calm and self-possessed, Lauren shaky and nervous.

'We're always bumping into each other,' he remarked.

'Yes.' In her thoughts she had had a hundred

conversations with him, but now that he was actually talking to her she couldn't think of a thing to say. Her mind was a vacuum. His effect on her was truly frightening.

'Coincidence, do you think?' he asked casually.

She had no idea what happened to her. Something snapped when she heard those words and she experienced an instant hot rage.

'What else?' Her tone was vicious. She was amazed at the way she sounded, amazed at her uncharacteristic explosiveness. It must have been the strain of the last weeks, the humiliation of his ignoring her all the time.

Joel raised his eyebrows in cool surprise. 'What else indeed?'

His composure enraged her even more. 'Are you insinuating,' she asked acidly, 'that it isn't? That I *plan* to run into you everywhere?'

He shrugged. 'Do you?'

'No!' She nearly choked on the word. 'This is a small foreign community! People bump into each other all the time! If you think that I'm going around looking for you, you're out of your mind! Who the hell do you think you are?'

'You haven't figured it out yet?' He seemed amused.

She would have liked to slap his arrogant face. He was observing her as if she were something fascinating under a microscope. Well, she'd wanted him to pay attention to her, hadn't she? He was doing it now, and she didn't like it.

Lauren walked away without another word.

Next time she saw him they were at a large reception given by the Governor to celebrate the Indonesian day of independence. Along with all the local politicians and dignitaries, the entire foreign community had been invited. After going down the reception line and shaking hands with the Governor and his entourage, they were invited to partake of refreshments. Large tables were laid with plates full of Javanese delicacies and drinks of various kinds.

Joel stood right behind her with his plate.

'Hello, Lauren,' he said.

'Hello,' she returned coolly. She hadn't forgotten her outburst of a few days ago; she was sure he hadn't either. She fixed her eyes on the food, helping herself to some pigeons' eggs and some crispy *krupuk*, and hoping that her inner turmoil wouldn't show.

'Here we are again,' Joel commented conversationally.

She tried to keep her temper under control. 'You can't blame me for this one, can you?' she asked calmly. 'And I'd like to make note of the fact that *you* followed *me* in line.' With that she moved away from him, attaching herself to the group of people farthest away from him: Josie and Steve, Anne Furgeson passing on juicy gossip, a newly arrived Swiss couple.

Silently she listened to the talk, not really caring, feeling helpless and miserable. She longed for some kindness between them—just a smile or a friendly word. But there was only tension and anger, and she didn't understand it and she didn't want it.

She ate her food and drank a bottle of soda water. Her eyes swept the room, finding Joel on the other side, deeply engaged in conversation with a man she didn't know. By the way Joel held his head she could tell he was engrossed in what the man was saying.

It seemed strange, then, that suddenly he turned his head slightly and looked straight into her eyes, across the entire room, across all those many heads. A shock shivered through her. He held her glance for only a moment, but she was sure he had felt the current that had leaped up between them.

A two-hour entertainment programme followed. Lauren sat in the large air-conditioned hall and watched, seeing and hearing little. She examined the audience, the clothes people were wearing, the hairdos. The Javanese women wore batik *kain*, lengths of cloth wrapped around so tightly they could barely walk or sit. Their heavily made up faces were dusted with a light powder that looked rather ghostly, and their dark hair was swept up high with large intricately knotted hairpieces attached to the backs of their heads.

Her eyes kept going to Joel, sitting slightly to the left, three rows ahead of her.

There was something not real about him, as if he were merely playing a part. She didn't like this man. She didn't like the mask with which he presented himself to her. Behind the façade she sensed something else, a different nature, a different man. Someone intimately familiar.

The old melancholy sadness swept over her suddenly. Her vision blurred and his image was no longer sharply defined. What she wanted was there, but it was out of reach, hiding.

CHAPTER TWO

LAUREN tried to put Joel out of her mind. For reasons she couldn't begin to understand, thinking about him made her sad and depressed, and she had better things to do with her time.

On Saturday night she stayed home and started sewing a new dress.

On Sunday morning she baked a very complicated cake, using a French recipe, a dictionary and conversion tables. She didn't have a scale for weighing flour and sugar, so she had to convert grams into cups and spoons. Her gas oven sported numbers running from 1 to 8, but no degrees. She felt more like a mathematician than a cook and she was sure that somewhere along the line she'd made a mistake in the calculations and the cake would be a complete disaster.

It came out beautifully, which created a problem: what was she going to do with it?

The loneliness of the long empty Sunday stretched out before her like an endless grey wasteland. Lauren hated Sundays. All the married people were having fun with their spouses and children, and almost everybody, it seemed, was married. But when you were single and you'd baked a cake and read an entire book and cleaned out the desk drawers and written to your grandmother, what was left?

It was her own fault. What was she doing single at the age of twenty-seven? She should have been married ages ago, then she would now have an adoring husband and two lovely children. They'd eat her cake and tell her what a good cook she was and they'd all sit around the table playing board games or painting watercolour

pictures. Later they'd all go to the zoo and before going
to bed they'd gather around the baby grand piano and
sing happy songs.

Lauren sighed and gazed dispiritedly at the cake,
thinking with longing of her parental home. There had
never been a lack of people to eat whatever her mother
had concocted. Friends, neighbours and visitors were
always passing through. Everybody enjoyed being at
their house.

Her mother was one of those rare women who
manage to make a home for husband and children no
matter where they are. Though they had moved to a
different place every few years, their family life had
been marked by a stability and continuity of routine,
making the other changes in their lives less threatening
and destabilising.

So many memories. Of learning to cook and bake, of
painting on large canvases, of playing the piano, of all
of them singing together. What was she doing here, so
far away from the people she loved? She was suddenly
overwhelmed with longing for home, for her mother's
apple pie, for the smell of her father's pipe, for the
sound of their piano.

Her parents had settled in Iowa. Her brother and
sister had both married and moved away. Lauren was
the only one still flying free and she liked it most of
the time—she wasn't unhappy—but still she missed
the closeness of attachment to other people. Making
good friends was almost impossible the way she was
living, moving from one place to another every few
months, never settling, never even decorating the
places she lived in. She was, it seemed, perpetually
camping out.

Why had she chosen this lifestyle? It hadn't been
necessary. She could have had other jobs, more
stability, an apartment of her own with plants and
books and paintings on the walls. Had she stayed put,

she might have found a man she could love and marry. But she had only known fleeting relationships that had never had time to develop into more permanent arrangements.

There was a restlessness inside her that prevented her from settling down. Something spurred her on to keep moving, to keep looking for different things and different places, a restless, hurried searching for something she had never defined. She didn't know; it was more a feeling than a conscious knowing.

The telephone rang, and Lauren catapulted out of her chair as if she couldn't wait for the surprise awaiting her when she picked up the receiver. Maybe it was Joel wanting to make friends. Maybe somebody asking her for lunch, for dinner, anything.

It was Sten. Her heart dropped an inch from sheer disappointment.

'Do you hate Sundays as much as I hate Sundays?' he asked.

'I don't think I can answer that, not knowing how much you hate Sundays.'

'On a scale of one to ten, it's a ten.'

'All right, in that case I probably hate Sundays as much as you do.'

'I hoped you would.'

'You're so generous!'

'Well, you know what I mean. Do you know what I've been doing all morning?'

Lauren had no desire to find out. 'No. I'll tell you what I did all morning. I baked a cake.' It was sitting on the dining room table, oozing chocolate and cream, begging to be eaten. 'You wouldn't want to stop by and have a piece, would you?' she heard herself say. Oh, well, she couldn't let that cake grow sour and mouldy. Besides, Sten was harmless. He was lonely, just like she was. Maybe they could cheer each other up.

At any rate, she needed something to drag her out of

this mire of self-pity and melancholy. She would plan a party, make a true feast and gather around her a houseful of people. If she was going to be here for another nine months she might as well put some effort into making life less lonely.

'Do I want to stop by and have a piece of cake?' echoed Sten. 'Now what kind of question is that? I'll be over in five minutes flat!'

Lauren made coffee, cut the cake, gathered everything on a tray and took it outside to the living room verandah. She was sorry already for having asked him. It was a mistake. The last thing Sten needed was encouragement. Well, it was too late now.

She contemplated the green bean tree while she waited for him to show up. The lacy greenery was silhouetted delicately against the bright blue sky. Branches drooped heavily with gigantic seedpods, some bright green, others dried and brown. They resembled huge green beans, and since she didn't know the name of the tree, she privately called it the green bean tree.

When Sten arrived, he ate two pieces of cake and complained about his job for an entire hour. Lauren wrapped up half the remainder of the cake for him to take home to sustain his sweet tooth for the next two days.

She had a terrible time getting rid of him. The day was a washout.

She was glad the next day was Monday and she could go to the office and busy herself with the preparations for a trip she had to make in another week. She didn't even mind seeing Ed again and watching him comb his few hairs fastidiously across his bald spot. He combed his hair a lot. Lauren knew he had a hang-up about getting old.

Why were people so conscious of age? she wondered. Covering it up? Lying about it? Eradicating the signs of it? Face-lifts, nose jobs, buttock tucks, hair dye, silicone. What had happened to growing old gracefully?

It was what she planned to do: grow old gracefully. No dyeing of grey hair, plumping up of wrinkles, smoothing out of various body parts. Growing old, she told herself, was a natural process. Don't fool with Mother Nature. Wrinkles show character, tell the world this person *lived*.

Easy for her to say. She was twenty-seven and no signs of decay were as yet visible, although science maintained that her body had been in decline for two years now. After twenty-five, so she had read, the body starts to disintegrate slowly and it's all downhill from there.

So far so good. But who could really know how she would feel when the first ravages of age would show in the mirror? The first grey hair might send her streaking to the beauty parlour. Who was she to pass judgment? Wait till you're thirty-five, Lauren Carmichael, she told herself, and see what you'll do when you see your face shrivelling up before your very eyes. A new wrinkle every day to show the world you *lived*.

Lauren worked in a frenzy all day, starting at seven in the morning and arriving home a little after three. Offices closed early in Semarang. A piece of cake was begging to be eaten, so she obliged, pouring a cold drink to go with it. Yanti was out somewhere and the house was quiet as a tomb.

The telephone shrilled through the silence.

Sten, again.

'Are you going to the Hash?' he enquired. 'You haven't been for weeks.' He sounded quite accusatory.

'I've been busy.'

'You're home now. Are you coming?'

'I was considering it.'

Lauren had joined the Hash House Harriers, a loosely organised, independent running club, soon after she had arrived in Indonesia. In Semarang a group run was organised every Monday afternoon. A trail was

laid with strips of coloured paper somewhere out of
town, though cassava plots and past rice paddies, up
and down hills and across little streams. Permission was
always asked of the villagers, who would gather to watch
and laugh at the runners.

'It's a good run today,' said Sten. 'The Dutch are
laying it, so be prepared.'

The Dutch had the reputation of laying the longest,
most tortuous trails. Lauren didn't mind; she liked the
exercise. A couple of days a week she got up early and
jogged around the Governor's mansion a few times,
doing about three miles, supplying the local populace
with free entertainment.

'All right,' she said, 'I'll go.'

'Good. I'll pick you up in half an hour. It's quite far
out of town, so we might as well go together and save
gas.'

Save gas, hah!

'As long as you keep your hands on the steering wheel
and not on my knee,' she cautioned.

He grinned audibly. 'You have such lovely knees.
When you wear shorts you're irresistible.'

'You're a lecherous old man, Sten. It's high time that
wife of yours came back. If I were her I wouldn't trust
you alone for a day!'

'I've been very good!' He sounded indignant.

'Keep it that way.' Sten was a lot of talk and no
substance. If she had ever taken him up on his offer of
nocturnal passion he would run like a frightened rabbit.
She thought so, anyway. Of course she couldn't be sure.

He sighed. 'I'll see you in a little bit.'

Most runners were there already when they arrived
and the *Anker Bir* truck was standing by with crates of
beer and soft drinks. From a nearby village children
and young people had gathered to watch the spectacle.
They had formed a circle around the Hashers and
inched closer and closer, goggling at them with large

brown eyes and giggling and laughing and saying things
to each other in Javanese which none of the foreigners
could understand.

Before Lauren had even seen him, she could sense
Joel was there. It was the most extraordinary feeling,
this knowing without knowing. Searching the crowd,
she noticed him leaning against the truck, drinking a
beer and talking to a German who worked on the
construction of a power generation plant.

Her heart began to beat erratically and her knees
turned to water. Why could she never stay cool in his
presence? He looked like a picture in a sports
magazine—healthy and brown and full of vigour and
virility. He wore blue running shorts, white sports shoes
and a white shirt. Around his head he had a green
sweatband. The green and the blue clashed, which
pleased her. She liked men wearing nice clothes, but
there was such a thing as overdoing it. At least Joel
wasn't too fastidious.

He noticed her when she came forward to get a bottle
of soda water. He gave her a slight nod in greeting,
raising his eyebrows as if he was surprised to see her.
She wondered why.

The Hash Master was a tall, blond Australian who
spoke a chewy English and had a great enthusiasm for
swear words of the most colourful variety, and an even
greater love for the singing of raunchy songs. Lauren
had finished her drink when he blew his horn to signify
the start of the run and everyone took off in a mad
dash.

Lauren was behind the bulk of them, wanting to stay
out of Joel's view. It was difficult going and her eyes
kept darting from the scenery back to the trail in front
of her to make sure she wasn't going to twist an ankle on
the dry rutted soil or on some fallen branch. It seemed
amazing that, despite the drought that had lasted for
months now, crops were still growing. Cassava plants

stood high and green. The terraced rice paddies shone bright as jade and emeralds. Apparently the mountain streams still supplied water for irrigation.

She crossed a small stream where women and children were sitting on rocks, bathing and washing clothes. They watched her wide-eyed as she jumped across to the other side.

'*Selamat sore,*' she greeted them, and their faces broke into smiles as they repeated the greeting.

A small bunch of paper strips directed her to a hill and she climbed up, the blood pounding in her head from heat and exertion. She had lost the rest of the group and saw no one for at least half a mile. But the paper guided her and she kept going on.

Then she was lost. There was no more paper anywhere, and no other runners. Standing in the shade of a clump of banana plants, she wiped her face and tried to catch her breath. She searched around in every direction, but without success. No paper, no people. She pondered the situation.

On the horizon, the sun was sinking, streaking the sky lavender and pink and peach. At her feet the rough terrain threatened her with its clumps of dried earth, roots and sticks and other hidden dangers.

She should have stayed with somebody. It was never a good idea to take off on your own.

If she broke a leg who could tell how long it would take them to find her? She wasn't on the trail any more. Her mind produced visions of her lying on the hard ground writhing in pain while the dark crouched over her and search parties looked for her in vain.

Hungry and thirsty and semi-conscious, she would wonder about gangrene setting in. Then, in the middle of the night, after she had given up all hope, voices would reach her ear. Through the swirling mists of semi-consciousness Joel's face would appear above her, white and worried and deathly tired.

'Darling, darling, I thought I'd never find you!' he would exclaim passionately, just like in old-fashioned love stories. He would kneel beside her, take her in his arms and tell her how much he loved her. Then blackness would engulf her and she would swoon delicately in his arms, her head trustingly on his shoulder.

She would come to. He would hold a cup of brandy to her lips and make her drink it. Only the *Anker Bir* truck did not carry brandy. Maybe he would give her beer. At any rate, he would look at her lovingly, telling her he had been terrified she would be lost for ever, or killed falling down a hill, or kidnapped by creatures from outer space. 'Oh, darling,' he would say, 'I didn't realise how much I loved you until you were lost! I was afraid I'd never see you alive to tell you. I would never have forgiven myself! Oh, darling, I've been so foolish—all the pain I've caused you! Please say you'll forgive me!'

She would forgive him, with tears of joy in her eyes. And they would live happily ever after.

Lauren sighed as she looked around the empty countryside. She'd never be so lucky. It would be Sten who would find her, sling her over his shoulder, broken leg and all, and carry her back to the others.

It would be better all the way around if she didn't break a leg. There was half an hour of light left. She might be lost, but she had a good sense of direction. If she climbed the hill to the left she would probably see the starting point and all the people and the cars and the truck.

She climbed the hill with aching legs and pounding heart and reaching the top she looked down across the fields below. She saw them then, the other Hashers, like little dolls way off in the distance. Carefully cutting across the fields, she ran and walked and jogged towards them, making sure not to trample the crops. A man wearing a conical hat was hoeing a patch of parched land by hand. He stopped and stared at her as she jogged past him.

Crazy foreigner, she could hear him think. It made her feel slightly guilty spending all this seemingly useless energy on a run, rather than doing something useful with it, such as hoeing a plot of land or harvesting rice.

She joined up with the others soon, and by the time they reached the parking area with the beer truck and their faithful audience, she was truly wiped out. Her legs wouldn't go an inch farther and, taking a beer, she staggered to a grassy bank and slumped down. Her face was hot and flushed, and her shirt and shorts were soaked through. And this, she said to herself, we do for fun. No wonder the villagers all think we're crazy!

Closing her eyes, she concentrated on calming her breathing and slowing down her heartbeat. Something prickled her senses and she opened her eyes. Joel stood in front of her, tall and overpowering, holding a beer.

'May I join you?' he asked.

Lauren couldn't believe her ears. He had actually searched her out!

'Be my guest,' she said, her voice carefully casual. 'As long as you realise that it's *you* who is joining *me*.'

'Touché.' There was humour in his voice and she could see his mouth faintly curling in a semblance of a smile. He sat down next to her, leaning his forearms on his pulled-up knees. His dark hair hung in damp strands on his forehead, sweatband gone. His clothes were as wet as hers.

He gave her an enquiring look. 'I hadn't expected to see you here,' he commented, taking a swig from his beer.

'Why not?'

'You didn't seem the type. Every time I see you, you're elegant, smooth and perfumed.'

Well, she certainly wasn't now. She said nothing.

'You must run regularly,' he remarked after a silence, glancing at her, then looking away towards the hills in the distance.

'Two or three times a week. I jog, really.'

They talked about running for a while, an innocuous conversation, but a conversation nonetheless. The first talk they had ever had that deserved that description, going beyond a mere three or four sentences. Lauren told him she usually jogged around the Governor's mansion a few times and that on Sundays she sometimes went to the track at the university.

'I'm getting used to the ridicule of the locals. They don't think I know how to run fast, and seeing a female in shorts is always good for some nasty comments.'

'This is a Muslim country,' Joel reminded her.

Lauren laughed. 'Statistically, yes. It doesn't go very deep for many. They like their beer and their cigarettes and women drive cars, and they don't segregate the sexes in schools and offices. Very decadent, if you ask me. Schoolgirls do sports in shorts too, so what's so funny about me?'

'You're eight inches taller than most and you're a foreigner.'

Over the top of the nearest hill they saw the last of the Hashers come trotting back. The sun hung like a fat orange balloon in the sky. The landscape was full of shadows and fading colours. A breeze touched Lauren's wet skin and she was almost cold. They sat in silence, sipping the last of their beers. Joel's face was silhouetted against the darkening sky and covertly she examined the strong profile, her eyes moving along the clean lines from forehead to nose to mouth to chin. Had she seen it somewhere before? That square chin? That straight nose? She groped around in the obscure labyrinth of her memory. Was it perhaps the resemblance to some famous person? A picture she had seen in a magazine? On TV? An image stored in the vast vaults of the unconscious?

Wouldn't it be wonderful if she would suddenly remember? If she could say, 'Oh, but you're the famous poet (pianist, pigeon trainer, palm reader)! I saw you on television! I've always admired your work!'

But it wasn't that, and she knew it. She kept returning to the simple explanation of familiarity of appearance because it was acceptable and understandable. And she wanted it to be that. She didn't like the mystic feeling of connection she sensed every time she was near him, or even just thought about him. It was beyond words and beyond reason, and it made her uneasy. Like an unexplained sound in an empty house in the dark of night.

She looked at his brown legs covered with dark hair, the ankles wrapped in white socks now reddish with dust. The legs of an athlete, strong and straight and muscled.

The Hash Master gave an ugly howl and shouted something she couldn't make out. Joel came to his feet in one smooth fluid movement and reached his hand out to pull her up. He had a grasp of iron and the contact shivered through her. He let go of her immediately and she glanced at his face, but it was without expression. Another first: the first time they had touched. We've never even shaken hands, she thought. We're making progress.

The ritual of the down-down began—the drinking of beer and the singing of bawdy songs and the emptying of beer mugs over heads. Beer was supposed to be good for your hair, but Lauren preferred to do without, although in previous weeks she had had her turns too. She watched and listened on the sidelines. Joel, as a newcomer, was awarded his very own down-down, complete with a song especially for the occasion. He stood in the circle of Hashers, gulping down a fresh beer to the admonishing chant of 'drink it down-down-down-down-down . . . .' By the time the chanting was finished, his beer was not, and he turned the mug upside down over his head and the remainder foamed over his hair and face, seeping into his shirt.

'You guys are just like a bunch of overgrown kids,' she couldn't help saying when it was all over. 'You'll fit right in here!' Her voice sounded slightly patronising, which she had intended.

Joel raised his eyebrows. 'Anything wrong with being a kid?'

She shrugged. 'I suppose it's harmless,' she said condescendingly. She watched carefully for his expression, but it didn't change.

'A little innocent fun is probably quite therapeutic.'

Lauren grimaced. 'Fun? Beer in your hair?'

'It's very refreshing,' he said evenly.

He was not to be provoked, that was obvious. She didn't understand why she even tried. She wasn't really one of those females who take great pleasure in goading men for no good reason at all.

Joel was so impassive and self-possessed that it was impossible to gauge the true state of his emotions—he seemed to have them perfectly under control. So far she hadn't seen much variation in his expression. His eyes were hard to read most of the time and it was difficult to measure him up.

Still, by instinct or intuition, she sensed behind that calm façade a passionate person. She wondered for whom he reserved the more ardent side of his nature— clearly it wasn't her. She didn't seem to stir in him any warm-blooded sentiments despite the fact that the currents were flowing hot and strong between them whenever they were together.

'Would you like another beer?' Joel asked, changing the subject.

'No, thanks—one's enough for me. I'll have a soda water, though.'

Bottles were handed down from the truck.

'I met that boss of yours a couple of days ago,' said Joel between swallows of beer. 'Strange character. How did you get saddled with him?'

'They put a contract in front of me and handed me my plane tickets. I mean, what could I do? It was either that or dire poverty in Bethesda, Maryland.'

'Is that where you're from?'

'In a manner of speaking. I have a friend who has an apartment there and she puts me up when I'm between jobs. That way I don't have to languish in some cheap hotel in Washington with little cards on the bedside table with a number to dial if I want the pleasures of a massage in the privacy of my own room.'

'I believe those are meant for the male of the species.' Joel grinned, showing strong white teeth, very straight. Probably regulated when he was a kid by a pound of gleaming steel clamped in his mouth, she thought.

'The world is very male-orientated,' she couldn't refrain from saying.

'You seem to be holding your own quite well in this male-orientated world,' Joel observed.

'I have to contend with male chauvinists like Ed.'

'He didn't seem *that* bad to me.'

'You're a man,' she said meaningfully.

Eyes slightly narrowed, he scrutinised her face. 'Tell me,' he said casually, 'you're not a Women's Lib fanatic, are you?'

'Fanatic? No, I don't believe so. But a few more months with Ed just might make me one.'

'What does he do that's so terrible?'

'He doesn't take women seriously. He keeps telling me that all a woman needs in this world is a good man in her bed. Preferably someone as virile as he.' She added the last sentence with a good dose of sarcasm. Of course Ed had never actually said that, but knowing Ed she knew that was what had been implied.

Joel laughed out loud. 'He seems to think a lot of himself, but it's a poor show.'

Lauren made a face. 'Tell me that deep down Ed harbours enough insecurity and feelings of inferiority to fill the National Archives.'

'You've got it.'

'I came to that conclusion a long time ago, but it doesn't help a bit.'

Sten appeared at her side with a pained expression. 'Are you ready to go?' he asked.

Lauren looked at his foot. 'Did you hurt yourself?'

'I tripped,' he growled. 'Damn near broke my ankle!' He limped off in the direction of his Mitsubishi Colt. It didn't look too bad. Saying goodbye to Joel, Lauren followed Sten to the car.

The entire way back she had to listen to Sten cursing the Dutchmen who had laid the treacherous trail. He sounded like a little boy, and she was glad when they arrived at her gate.

She soaked her battered body in a tub of cool, soapy water, sipping a large Campari and soda. It had become her after-Hash ritual: a bubble bath and a Campari. It was the only time she ever indulged in solitary drinking.

Yanti had fixed her a dinner of potato salad and cold fried chicken, and she ate everything on the table, which was considerable. Yanti made sure she never went hungry. Lauren retreated to the living room where the overhead fan stirred feebly and turned it up full speed, sending some loose papers flying across the room. They were survey forms she had been working on at home, and with a sigh she gathered them up and stuck them under a book to keep them from flying off again. She picked up a novel she had started the day before and waited for Yanti to bring her her *kopi tubruk*.

With a little bit of luck the coffee would keep her awake till nine or nine-thirty, so she could go to bed at a halfway respectable time. The thought occurred to her that there had been times in the past when she had gone to bed routinely at eleven or later. Nowadays, if she could stay awake till ten it was a miracle. Maybe she was turning into an old maid. She certainly wasn't attracting a lot of attention from Joel, and she had never before had trouble getting men interested in her if she gave them half a chance. Maybe she was past her peak.

The thought was so demoralising that she could feel her body droop with depression. She gripped her book with both hands, gritted her teeth, and glued her eyes to the printed page.

Five minutes later, her fingers cramped, her jaws locked, she realised she was holding the book upside down.

Joel was stacking beer cans in a shopping cart next time she saw him. She had come straight from the office to Galael's to buy some groceries. She had just picked up a plastic bag of eggs, reminding herself for the umpteenth time to look into the possibility of an egg carton factory, when she noticed him at the end of the aisle. He raised his head immediately and glanced in her direction as if he had felt her eyes on him.

Her heart lurched. Oh, foolish, foolish heart! She could have turned her cart around and galloped off in another direction, but she didn't. Invisible strings were pulling her straight towards him. She was helpless. She continued down the aisle and it seemed he was waiting for her.

'Hello, Lauren.'

He was wearing blue slacks and a dark batik shirt and his grey eyes were almost transparent. If she'd look deep into those eyes, maybe she'd be able to see through them, like glass, straight into his hidden inner self. Of course she couldn't stand there in the middle of the supermarket staring into his soul. It just wasn't done.

'Hi,' she replied, letting her gaze slip away from him in feigned indifference and pretending to examine the soft drinks.

'Fascinating, aren't they?' His voice held amusement.

'Very.' She proceeded to take some cans of soda water off the shelf and put them in the cart. Without looking at him she swung into another aisle and continued her shopping. It took all her strength not to look back to see where he was going. A moment later he was right next to her. Her body tensed. He was holding two boxes of macaroni, two different brands.

'What do you think,' he said conversationally, 'this one or this one?'

Lauren shrugged. 'When it comes to macaroni, go by the price.'

He examined the figures written on the boxes with a felt-tipped pen. 'There's a twenty-rupiah difference. About two cents.'

'Now you know. Take the cheaper one.'

'I like the colour of the other box better.' He looked deadly serious.

'If that's worth two cents, by all means indulge yourself.' Lauren was utterly disgusted. The man was cracked! Leave it to her to feel attracted to someone who wasn't altogether straight in the head, someone who agonised over the colour of a box of macaroni.

Joel must have read her thoughts, because suddenly he grinned. 'Not two cents. *Millions*.'

She scanned his face. 'I have the feeling I'm missing something.'

His grin widened. 'I'm talking about marketing, packaging. I was reading an interesting article this morning about the problems of selling domestic products in foreign markets. It came to mind when I looked at the macaroni.' There were sparks of amusement in his eyes, 'Did you think I was off my rocker?'

'Yes.' She paused. 'Now we're even.'

He quirked an eyebrow. 'Did I ever say you were off your rocker?'

'You must have entertained the notion once or twice.'

'Not exactly.'

The tone of his voice did not reveal what notion exactly he *had* entertained about her, and she was too proud to ask. Besides, it might be something worse, and why should she expose her ego to unnecessary abuse?

Joel did not elaborate of his own accord and Lauren directed her attention to a package of cornflour. The box was yellow and red and didn't appeal to her in the least, which, at this particular moment, was of no consequence whatsoever, since she didn't need cornflour.

'Well, I'm done,' he said, dropping one of the boxes of macaroni in his cart and replacing the other one on the shelf. 'I'll see you.'

''Bye.' Lauren felt her body relax as she watched him march over to one of the two cash registers with his cart containing the beer and the macaroni as well as a bottle of Scotch and matches and butter and eggs and mayonnaise and breakfast cereal. Not a very revealing batch of groceries.

As she stared at his retreating back she wondered for the hundredth time what he really thought of her. She had not the faintest idea, but the fact that she pondered the question so often was cause for worry. Normally she wasn't excessively concerned about other people's opinion of her.

How *did* other people see her? She tried to visualise herself as a stranger, get out of her body, so to speak, and observe herself as others would.

Was she a career woman? An old maid? A swinging single?

A career woman, yes, she supposed so. An old maid?

She was twenty-seven and unmarried and she wore glasses. Fashionable ones, to be sure, but spectacles just the same. But she did not wear sensible shoes and her skirts were not too long and her mouth was not prim and proper and she did not hate men. On closer examination, then, she was not an old maid, which was reassuring. Was she a swinging single? She wasn't a swinger. She didn't drift from bed to bed or from man to man. She'd had a few flings, yes, but they'd not proved very satisfactory. Serious relationships took time and patience and enormous amounts of emotional investment, and Lauren didn't expose her inner self very easily. Her heart did not come cheap.

She couldn't decide on a category, which was just as well. Maybe others couldn't either. The idea of fitting a stereotype image was depressing. It robbed you of your individuality. She didn't like labels, boxes, boxes with labels.

A sigh escaped her. Here she was standing in the middle of Galael's, amid the smells of detergent and warm bread and cardboard, philosophising. What was the matter with her?

She pushed the cart over to the cash register. Joel had gone.

'Selamat sore,' she said, and the cashier smiled prettily and repeated the greeting. The girls were all so sweet and innocent-looking with their slim flat bodies and their narrow hips and their shy smiles. Smooth complexions, beautiful dark eyes, shiny black hair—they had it all.

'Thirty-three thousand four hundred and fifty rupiahs,' said the girl after she had rung up the groceries. In the beginning it had been a shock to see the amounts run into the thousands, and Lauren had to remind herself every time that one thousand rupiahs was only about one dollar.

The groceries were packed into flimsy baskets and

tied with pink string from a huge roll. Someone carried them to the car for her while she took the eggs and gingerly placed them on the seat next to her.

As she drove home she wondered how she actually saw herself.

She considered herself competent, self-sufficient, reliable, and not overly emotional, at least not to the naked eye. Granted, she blew up now and then, but it wasn't a daily habit. Apart from that she thought of herself as a romantic. Nobody liked candles, wine, soft music and moonlight more than she. She loved receiving flowers, schmaltzy cards and little love notes. Once she had received a poem and she had walked on clouds for days afterward.

Her idea of love and marriage was something totally unrealistic. It was a dream of everlasting happiness that had no relation whatsoever to the state of affairs she witnessed around her. In this fairyland fantasy she was never angry or miserable or insecure. The sun always shone. Her husband was always loving and kind and understanding. There was heavenly music all the time and soft summer breezes. The food was always delicious. Nothing ever went wrong. Potatoes never burned, people never got killed in car accidents.

A very juvenile fantasy, indeed, but not one she was likely to divulge to anyone. Someone her age who had seen what went on in the world in reality had no business dreaming about perfect happiness. But on the other hand, if she couldn't even fantasise about it, what was the use of getting out of bed in the morning?

With her Indonesian assistant, Tiur, Lauren went on a three-day field trial the following week. They travelled through small towns and villages and watched women making pots and baskets and *batik tulis*. They visited a batik workshop and observed the time-consuming process of producing handmade batik cloth.

In a dingy, badly lighted room, women were sitting on low stools in front of wooden frames that had lengths of cloth hung over them. The women drew intricate designs on the fabric in hot wax using a small tool made of brass and bamboo. Lauren was fascinated by their skill and the precision of their work. On the floor next to each woman stood a pan of hot wax on top of a charcoal burner.

After the waxing, the cloth was soaked in a cold water dye bath. The dyeing was a messy business that was done outside in the open, carried out by men only. Barefoot, they stirred the fabric around in shallow pans, lifting it with long poles from pan to pan. Lauren stood aside trying not to get splashed with dye and end up with a polka-dot design all over her.

The dye bath was followed by another waxing, then another dye bath, and the process was repeated until all the desired colours had been obtained. Then the wax was removed by boiling the cloth in water, and a design of incredible beauty would appear.

The waxing was hot and tedious work. For hours on end the women sat in the same position, their eyes trained on the fabric in front of them. Covers draped over their laps and legs prevented burns from dripping wax, but did nothing for staying cool in the already hot and cramped working space. Smells of hot wax filled the steamy air. It was a relief to be outside again.

Lauren knew that the final product of all this intense labour, the piece of *batik tulis*, or handmade batik, would sell for a high price. The women who did the tedious art work received less than a dollar a day. Lauren was used to seeing this sort of thing, but it still made her angry to see poor people slave all day for next to nothing while someone else made good money from their labour.

The highlight of her trip was a toothless old woman

who ran her own small palm sugar business. She lived in a mountain village in a very clean and neat little house that was painted your basic blue. The wooden window frames and the door were a bright green and the low wall around the verandah was a brave pink. Here was someone with a zest for living!

Teeth or no, Ibu Sajono smiled and laughed all the time, and her dark eyes were full of humour. Her greying hair was pulled back into a bun and she wore traditional clothes, including the *kain*, an ankle-length wrap-around skirt. She served Tiur and Lauren hot sweet tea in a glass and talked with enthusiasm about her business. The enthusiasm was easy to understand, but not the words, since she spoke in Javanese. Tiur made a valiant effort to translate everything into Indonesian, but keeping up with the old lady was no small task.

The little house was surrounded by coconut palms, the blooms of which produced the sap that was boiled down into sugar. They watched the woman's grandson walk up the trees (he didn't climb, he walked), sticking his toes into notches cut out in the trunks of the palms. Carrying several bamboo cups attached to a belt around his waist, he collected the sticky liquid, came down again and started up another.

Ibu Sajono proudly showed them the Lorena woodstove in her outdoor kitchen where she boiled down the sap to make the sugar. It was a light brown, very sweet sugar with a nice caramel-like flavour. She gave both of them a small cake of it to take home.

Lauren thought about the woman all the way home. Ibu Sajono didn't make very much money, but it was so much better to see a person in charge of her own life, someone who had some independence. Seeing the old lady cheered her up.

It always bothered her to come home to an empty house after she had been on a trip. No one to talk to. No one to share her adventures with. But fortunately she was usually too exhausted to dwell on it for long. Sleep would claim her as soon as she stretched her aching limbs on the mattress.

The Saturday after she returned she saw Joel again at a small dinner party. The house overlooked the town and she was contemplating the lights as she sipped a drink when he appeared next to her.

'Nice view,' he commented.

'Yes.' She hadn't seen him for over a week and she felt a thrill of nervous excitement. She glanced at him, then looked away again. He was leaning casually against the railing, one hand in his pocket, the other holding a glass. He was observing her.

She had the overwhelming urge to touch him. She closed her eyes, feeling dazed, then opened them again and fixed them on the town lights. The overpowering attraction she felt was truly frightening. She had a vision of Joel holding her, kissing her, making love to her.

Her hands were shaking so badly that her glass slipped from her fingers and crashed down below in a cement gutter, splintering into a thousand pieces.

He started. 'My God,' he muttered, and his hand came out and touched her arm, and a current shot through her. He gazed at her, frowning, removing his hand as if he had burned himself.

'Are you all right?'

'Yes,' she said for the second time. Her conversation was positively brilliant. 'My glass slipped out of my hand, that's all.' She turned, wanting only to get away now, away from him, out of the dark. But he followed her and they entered the house together.

Dinner was ready, and Joel was seated next to Lauren. She wasn't surprised any more. She only

hoped she could calm down enough to swallow her
food.

'Tell me about your field trip,' said Joel, spooning
avocado vinaigrette.

Everybody seemed interested, so she told them about
her experiences and a stimulating conversation followed.
After dessert, coffee was served on the verandah and
Joel sat down next to her. They talked for a long time,
and to her surprise it was easy and natural. Maybe the
wine had relaxed her a little. There was a harmony in
their thoughts and ideas that she had not expected. It
made her happy.

They left the house together. Their cars were parked
next to each other—twin Toyotas.

It was very dark and suddenly she didn't feel at ease
any longer. As if by magic, everything had changed
and she was aware of a tension quivering between
them.

She put her key in the car door. Joel's hand came
down on hers and again his touch went like an electric
shock through her arm. This time he did not withdraw
his hand but left it curling around hers. She looked at
it, not daring to lift her face to meet his eyes.

'Tell me,' he said in a voice that sounded strained,
'where do you think we've met before?'

Lauren couldn't speak. It was the last thing she had
expected him to say. Where did she think they'd met?
She didn't know the answer.

She raised her head and looked up into the deep inky
blue expanse of sky. The stars were blinding sparks of
light. In the far recesses of her memory something
stirred. She closed her eyes, but the stars were still there
and the darkness of the night sky, but it was not the
same sky and not the same night. She smelled the
fragrance of orange blossoms, felt a soft warm breeze
touch her skin, heard the voice of a man, a deep
resonant voice that reverberated in her mind. The old

familiar sadness washed over her and she wanted to cry, but not a sound stirred the stillness.

'Where? Do you remember where?' Joel's voice came from far away and she opened her eyes, reaching shakily for the car to give her support.

'Spain.' Her voice was nothing but a weak whisper and she was terrified by the sense of unreality that surrounded her. *What's happening to me?* she thought wildly.

Finally she looked up at him. His gaze was fixed on her intently. Please, she said wordlessly, don't look at me like that. We're not strangers.

Silence.

'Are you sure?' he asked at last.

She nodded. 'Yes, I'm sure.'

There was a slight pause. 'I've never been to Spain,' he said then.

Lying in bed later, Lauren couldn't remember how she had made it home. She couldn't remember coming into the house, taking off her clothes.

She couldn't sleep.

Spain. Why had she said Spain?

She was a Navy brat, had been hauled around the globe half a dozen times. She'd lived and travelled in countless places.

But Spain wasn't one of them.

She'd never set foot on Spanish soil, either.

CHAPTER THREE

SPAIN. The word kept echoing in her mind like a broken record and it wouldn't leave her alone. She thought about it at breakfast, lunch, dinner, and in between. There had to be a reason why she had mentioned Spain. What could possibly be the connection between Joel and her—a connection that had to do with Spain? As far as she could remember she had never even landed in Madrid for a fuelling stop or a transfer. Of course, as a child she wouldn't have known where she was.

She'd never been particularly interested in Spain. She hadn't even read Michener's *Iberia* and Hemingway's *For Whom the Bell Tolls*, which she had to admit was a lack in her education.

Her knowledge of the country was pitifully meagre—sherry, oranges, paella, bullfights and flamenco dancing about summed it up. She must have met the occasional Spaniard in her wanderings around the world, but she certainly didn't remember any.

Something strange was going on in her mind. How could she feel and think and remember things that had no roots in reality? How could she possibly feel these strong bonds with a man she had never met before?

Lauren hoped desperately that sooner or later a ray of understanding would penetrate the clouds around her memory—preferably before she began to doubt her sensibilities. She was sure that by now Joel Rockwell was convinced she had become unhinged. He wasn't ignoring her any more, probably because he had decided she was a harmless neurotic suffering from delusions.

Joel was in Jakarta for a few days, and Lauren stayed

home most of that next week. She didn't see him at all, which didn't prevent her from thinking about him almost constantly. It was not a reassuring sign.

On Saturday she gave a big party and invited everybody she knew. It occurred to her that people would expect Joel to be present. He was the new man in town and he was her neighbour. She'd have to invite him whether she wanted to or not.

She wanted to.

I probably won't have a moment's peace, she thought.

She sent Yanti with a note, inviting him, and he accepted with a few polite words scrawled on the paper underneath her own. Lauren liked his bold handwriting. She liked his face and his hands and his back. Trouble was looming large.

With Yanti's help she prepared a feast. The table was laden with aromatic Indonesian dishes, some very spicy, some not. She had concocted several gigantic fruit salads, using all the exotic local fruits, and soaked them in Grand Marnier mixed with pineapple juice.

The flower vendor, complete with his black pillbox hat and his perpetual smile, made a propitious appearance at her door that morning, carrying his enormous baskets on a bamboo pole across his shoulders. Lauren bought masses of flowers and probably made his week. She had bought flowers from him only a couple of times, but always for others. It was too depressing to buy flowers for yourself. At her age you should have a man or men doing it for you.

She spent a long time getting ready. Her slinky white dress made her look a lot cooler than she actually felt. Putting up her hair seemed to add another inch or so to her height, but no matter. There were definite advantages to being tall. Slipping on high-heeled sandals, she added some more.

She sensed Joel's arrival the moment he set foot in the door, which had been left open to admit the invited, most of whom were already there. His presence set off a sparkle in her awareness and she turned around. He was standing near the doorway, his gaze sweeping the room. Their eyes met, like two planes crashing in mid-air, and Lauren forgot to breathe. What was it about that face, those calm grey eyes, that made her react so violently? Why were her senses aware of him before she even knew he was there? A shiver of apprehension ran down her spine. She was beginning to feel spooked.

Joel came towards her with long, easy strides and her heart began to hammer against her ribs. There was nothing spectacular about the way he was dressed—light slacks and an open-necked batik shirt—but he was the most fascinating man she had ever seen. She liked the way he moved, the way he held his body, the way he coolly glanced around a room.

In his left hand he carried a bunch of flowers.

He handed them to her. 'Well,' he said, smiling faintly, 'it doesn't look as if you need these. It appears the flower man came to see you too.'

She managed a grin as she took the flowers from him. 'There's always room for more. No lack of empty jars!' All the flowers had been arranged in tin cans and glass jars as she did not own any vases, but the bright profusion of colour seemed to suffer none for the lack.

She sniffed the white, fragrant blooms. 'They smell delicious.' She wondered if he knew that what he had given her were traditional funeral flowers. It didn't seem diplomatic to point it out. 'I'll take care of these right now. Have a drink—the bar is over there in the corner. I'll be back in a minute and introduce you to the people you haven't met yet.'

She swept off to the kitchen, found another can of approximately the right size and arranged the flowers in it. Depression washed over her. Here was the first man she'd been interested in for quite some time, and he brought her *funeral* flowers!

Was it symbolic? A dead-end relationship. Love destined to perish.

It was utterly childish. She had bought the same flowers that very morning. In the Western world, in her own culture, these flowers had no connotation of death and funerals and mourning. They were nothing more than beautiful blooms that permeated a room with their perfumy fragrance. They appeared in vases in every expatriate house. Joel had bought them because they were the nicest flowers; that was all there was to it. Her morbid thoughts were ludicrous and silly.

She put the flowers on the bar. Joel was talking to Sten.

'Mmm, nice,' said Sten, looking at the flowers. 'They smell lovely.' His eyes roved over Lauren hungrily. 'Like you,' he added with a lascivious grin.

'Shut up, Sten,' she shot back, grimacing at Joel. 'His wife's in Denmark for a while. Turns him into a lecher!'

The party was a great success. The food was ambrosial, the conversation stimulating, the night romantic and her mood elated. It was well past one o'clock when the last people left, Joel among them. Yawning, and suddenly assaulted by mountainous waves of fatigue, Lauren staggered to her bedroom. Opening the door, she turned on the light and froze.

Sprawled out on the bed, fully dressed and fast asleep, lay Sten.

Anger raced hotly through her. A joke was fine, but this was going a little too far. She didn't want him in her bed, dressed or not. She shook him with determination, but he hardly stirred, murmuring something unintelligible. He was out cold. Lauren shouted in his ear and shook him some more. The result was unimpressive. He turned his face away and went right on sleeping. She considered pouring a glass of ice water over his face, but rejected the idea. Sleeping in a wet bed didn't appeal to her.

An alternative was to leave him right where he was and for her to sleep in the spare bedroom, but the bed wasn't made up and the room had no air-conditioning and she'd be damned if she'd allow an univited male to push her out of her own bed.

Without further deliberation she went to the phone and dialled Joel's number. He'd only just left, so she assumed he wouldn't be asleep yet.

He sounded surprised to hear her voice.

'I have a problem,' she said matter-of-factly.

'At one-thirty in the morning?'

'There's a man in my bed, and. . . .'

He laughed. 'And that's a problem?'

Lauren gritted her teeth. 'Under the circumstances, yes. He wasn't invited.'

'Let me guess. Sten?'

'Yes.'

'How did he get there?'

'He opened the door, waltzed in and collapsed on the bed!' Her voice carried a clear note of exasperation.

'Sorry,' he said easily, 'dumb question.'

'He's out cold—too much of that revolting concoction he mixes up for himself, no doubt. I couldn't wake him up and I can't move him and. . . .'

'I'll come and rescue the maiden in distress,' he interrupted. 'I'll be there in one minute.'

He was there in half.

'What do you want me to do with him?' Lauren's one-man rescue squad was all business.

'I don't care. You can dump him in the back of his car or in the garage. . . .'

Joel whistled between his teeth. 'You're a real sweetheart, aren't you?'

'I have no mercy on uninvited bed partners,' she said coldly.

Joel looked down on the peacefully sleeping shape on the bed and her gaze followed his. Sten was snoring, his mouth hanging open. One hand lay on his chest in the general vicinity of his heart as if to convince them of his innocence. The rest of his limbs lay on the bed in strangely contorted angles, positions she had not considered possible for the human body. He looked very uncomfortable and totally ridiculous.

'Prince Charming,' commented Joel.

Lauren suppressed a laugh. 'I'll get a sheet and put it on the bed in the room across the hall. You can put him in there if you think you can get him there.'

Joel bent over and slung the slack figure over his shoulder as if it were a sack of sand. It was hot in the room, and after she had spread out the sheet on the mattress and Joel had dumped Sten down on the bed, she went to get the portable fan.

When she got back Joel was pulling off Sten's shoes, and together they took care of the rest of his clothes. He lay there, smooth-chested and wearing only dark blue under-shorts, looking innocent as a little boy.

'I don't believe he'll give you any trouble for a while,' said Joel, and he adjusted the fan in Sten's direction. 'When is his wife coming back?'

'Next week.'

'I hope you can hold out.' His voice was dry.

'Hold out? Me? I can handle him. I just won't let him back in the house and near the bar.'

They left the room and Joel closed the door behind him. In the living room and dining room the party's debris lay angrily waiting to be cleared away. Lauren had sent Yanti away earlier in the evening and the girl intended to recruit her sister to help put the place back together in the morning.

Dirty glasses glowered at her accusingly. Left-over food lay drying up on the plates. Furniture glared at her from all the wrong places. Overflowing ashtrays wafted their stale, smoky smell through the air. Crumpled napkins lay on the floor, begging for disposal.

Joel surveyed the wreckage as they passed. 'I was under the impression we were having a civilised party,' he said with a note of irony.

'You wouldn't think so looking at this mess. You'd think the Vandals had come through and sacked the place!'

'Cleaning this up is going to be a massive undertaking. Would you like a hand?'

'No, thanks. Yanti is bringing reinforcements in the morning. I refuse to worry about it.'

He grinned. 'A very healthy attitude.'

Lauren walked out of the front door with him into the starry night and realised that she was no longer tired. She wanted more than anything for Joel to stay, to be alone with him. She wanted to be near him and talk to him and listen to his voice and look at his face.

She wanted to be in his arms.

Please don't go home, she said silently. Please stay with me.

He stopped and looked at her. In the shadowy light of the moon she saw something flicker across his face, as if somehow he had heard her silent plea. Her heart beat in her throat and she had trouble breathing. She stood motionless, her eyes fixed on his face, wondering if it were possible for him to sense her feelings without her saying or doing anything. Her mind was in chaos.

A lizard *crock-crocked* nearby. Some nocturnal bird fluttered past overhead. A breeze rustled the palm fronds and stroked her skin. The night air was warm, but still she shivered. She had a strange sensation of unreality, of time standing still, of floating in endless space. The sparkling splendour of the starry sky seemed everywhere around her. A force inside her reached out to the man in front of her, and she felt the answering current quivering between them. A mysterious force was taking over, and she was filled with a sudden mystic sense of pre-destiny.

She had no awareness of moving, only of being in his arms, of feeling the muscled strength of his body against hers. There was a familiarity in the embrace, as if she had been in his arms many times before. A homecoming.

I belong to him, she thought in wonder. *We belong to each other*. The truth of it was radiant and eternal as the stars. Joel was her love and he had always been. He was the man she had always been waiting for.

She felt his kiss, the warmth of his mouth, his hands holding her face, and there was nothing but the two of them in the warm night, and the tenderness and the love and the passion that trembled through their clinging bodies.

It was a moment out of time, not part of earthly reality, for suddenly she heard his voice wishing her goodnight and she was no longer in his arms and he was striding down the path away from her. It seemed as if this mysterious moment of rapture had never happened at all.

Or did there exist, she wondered, some different sphere of consciousness?

It took her a long time to fall asleep.

Sten had the grace to be embarrassed when he emerged from the bedroom the next morning. He muttered some excuses about not having meant to fall asleep on her bed, about not having meant to lie down on her bed in the first place.

Lauren said nothing. She had no desire to let him off the hook too easily. With only a few hours of sleep she wasn't in the most generous of moods. She felt positively rotten. Sitting in the middle of all the cheerless flotsam and jetsam of the previous night's festivities did nothing for her state of mind.

The air was hot and muggy. Through the open window drifted the acrid smoke of a smelly fire; some ambitious person was burning a heap of garbage by the side of the road near her house. Sunday was as good a day as any, she guessed. Sweeping aside the dirty glasses and dishes from one end of the table, she cleared a space. She had rounded up some cups from under tables and chairs and washed them.

Sten looked sick. He probably had the hangover of all hangovers.

Silently Lauren poured him coffee. He gave her a pleading look which she pretended not to see. Let him suffer a little! She felt sorry for his wife who had to put up with this miserable excuse of a man.

You're overreacting, she said to herself as she sipped her coffee. There's nothing fundamentally wrong with the man except that his growing-up process screeched to a halt at the age of fourteen. He has the mental maturity of an adolescent. You should feel sorry for the wretched man.

Silently she considered this. She didn't have it in her. No mercy forthcoming from her. She gave it to him. How dared he go to her bedroom? How dared he lie down in *her* bed? Had he never heard of the word privacy? Did he not understand the word *no*? Had she not made it clear to him that she was not favourably disposed towards his juvenile advances? When was he going to grow up? What about his wife? What about the people who had left the party last night, seeing the one solitary Mitsubishi Colt staying behind in the driveway? Did he not know what the logical conclusion would be? What if word got back to his wife?

Sten looked like a beaten dog.

She fed him toast and poured more coffee. He left as soon as he had finished. Lauren watched him climb into the Colt, start up the engine, then kill it twice before he finally made it out the driveway.

She felt much better.

Five minutes after Sten had departed, Yanti and her

sister arrived, ready for Operation Clean-up. It seemed advantageous to get out of the way, so Lauren evacuated to the swimming pool at the Patra Jasa Hotel.

A hundred black-haired children clogged the pool and saturated the air with their shrieks of fear and delight. It was early Sunday morning and she should have known. She should have gone back to bed. Anyway, by ten-thirty or so peace would resume, as most of the children would have left by then.

There was no room in the pool to swim and no room in the shade to sit. She lay down in the sun hoping for something less than a third-degree burn. Of course she'd forgotten her tanning lotion. But she did have a book.

She read. When she got too hot she lowered herself carefully into the deep end of the pool and, battling the masses of kicking arms and legs, swam across a couple of times to cool off her burning flesh. Then she had a cool drink and read some more.

By eleven the place was practically deserted and she captured herself a wooden lounger in the shade. After she had taken a long, leisurely swim she parked herself contentedly on the lounger and closed her eyes. When she opened them after a while she noticed several people at the other side of the pool: Josie and Steve and some others. Then Joel appeared. He dumped his bag on a chair, stripped off his clothes and sauntered over to the deep end of the pool.

He wore black, European-style swimming trunks and his body looked magnificent standing there poised at the edge of the pool. He hadn't seen her, which gave her a good opportunity to watch him unobserved. He took a quick dive into the water, and a beautiful sight it was to see his sleek, tanned body slide through the air, then into the water. Lauren got up and casually strolled over to the edge of the pool and watched him swim, her stomach tightening. He was a superb swimmer, which didn't surprise her in the least. He was one of those superior men who can do it all. He could probably fly a plane, cut diamonds, scuba-dive, play the saxophone and build a ham radio.

She dived into the water and surfaced right next to him.

'Beautiful,' he said with a grin.

My dive or me? she wanted to know, but had the good sense not to voice the question. She swung her wet hair over her shoulders and smiled graciously.

'Did you get rid of your guest?' he asked, treading water next to her.

She told him what had happened. Then they swam some more before getting out to sit in the shade. There was an apple in her bag, but she didn't take it out. She would have liked to share it with him if she'd had a way of cutting it, but she didn't. It seemed to her that offering him bites was too intimate a suggestion in the bright light of the noon sun. He was friendly and relaxed but gave not a hint of acknowledgment of the romantic interlude under the starry sky of the previous evening. Maybe it had only been a fantasy, a product of her over-active imagination induced by her clamouring senses. All the spicy food creating havoc with the chemical balances in her brain.

So, leaving the apple in her bag, she asked him innocuous questions, making light conversation. What about his family? Did he have any brothers and sisters? Where did his parents live? Where had he grown up? She realised that in other circumstances she would be bored to tears. But they were talking about Joel and that made all the difference. He was the most intriguing man, and the fact that he had a brother and no sisters and parents who lived in Kansas City was exceedingly fascinating.

He had gone to university in San Diego, he told her.

'Do you like California?' she asked, hoping he didn't.

He nodded. 'I do, very much.'

Lauren didn't, but she said nothing.

He gave her a sideways glance with half-closed eyes. 'You look very disapproving.'

'I don't like California.'

'You're not the only one,' he said dryly.

'Besides that, it gives me the creeps. One more earthquake and it'll tear off and sink into the deep blue sea.'

'So I've heard.' He seemed unimpressed.

'Everything in California is fake and artificial,' she generalised with outrageous arrogance. She wondered if that would get him. Sweeping statements such as this one were usually good to get people all hot and bothered. They tended to get Lauren all hot and bothered. 'It's all so plastic and synthetic over there,' she added for good measure.

'That's why I'm not worried, you see. It won't sink. It'll just float away on the waves.'

Obviously Joel did not get hot and bothered.

He scrutinised her through half-closed eyes. 'And by the way, didn't they teach you in school that words such as *always* and *never* and *all* and *none* and *everything* are best avoided because they render most statements untrue and invalid?'

Lauren grinned. 'Touché!' She licked her index finger and wrote a mark in the sky. 'One for you.'

'You're a bit obvious, you know,' he said evenly.

'Obvious?' She looked innocent.

'Why are you trying to pick a fight with me?'

She sighed. 'You're so even-tempered. I'd like to find out what you're like when you're mad.'

Joel groaned. 'You women are all the same.'

'Ah! You said *all*!'

'It's one of the few exceptions to the rule.' He was unperturbed.

'I'm going to take another swim before I really get mad.' Lauren took off her glasses and put them on the table.

'Do. It'll cool you off.'

She ignored that. She took a deep dive, touched bottom and came back up. Joel had turned the game right around. Served her right, too. Not that she'd admit that to him. She swam a few laps, then climbed out of the water and sat down on her lounger.

Joel lay stretched out comfortably, eyes closed, hands behind his head. Lauren studied him through her lashes. Broad shoulders, chest matted with dark hair, narrow hips, hard-muscled legs. In his black swimming shorts he looked like someone in a magazine advertisement promoting luxury cruises, island vacations or superior rum.

'Have you ever done any modelling?' she asked.

He opened one eye. 'What?'

'Have you ever done any modelling? You know, for ads and commercials.'

'No.' Both eyes were open now and one corner of his mouth curled up in faint amusement. 'And you?'

She shrugged. 'Only a little, while I was in college. I did small jobs, local stuff. It helped financially.'

They started talking about the high cost of college education.

Josie came trotting over, squealing about her feet burning on the blistering cement. She crashed down at the foot of Lauren's lounger, face contorted with pain. She wore a blue and white striped swimsuit, the stripes running horizontally and accentuating her width which didn't need emphasising. Her thin, limp hair was glued wetly to her scalp, making her head look too small for her body.

She'd had a great time at the party, she said, gushing approval of the food, the music, the flowers, Lauren's sexy dress.

Lauren thanked her and tried to change the subject. It is nice to be admired, but too much is embarrassing. Josie started in on Lauren's swimsuit and her body in it and it was getting more awkward by the moment. She was uncomfortably aware of Joel and the curling corner of his mouth.

'You have to tell me how you do it,' Josie sighed.

'Do what?'

'Stay thin!'

'I'm just lucky, Josie. I don't get fat by looking at a carrot. But I do jog about nine miles a week. I suppose that helps.'

Josie giggled. 'I'd trip over my own feet! I'd start a riot in the streets here. The Indonesians would die laughing if they saw me bouncing down the road!'

'They laugh at me too. They shout all kinds of things at me in Javanese, obscenities, I'm sure, but I don't understand it, so I don't let it bother me.'

Josie stared at her left big toe. 'I suppose,' she said reflectively, 'I could start drinking water instead of soft drinks and cut out desserts and the sugar in my coffee and give up cakes and cookies.'

'It would help,' Lauren said encouragingly. She didn't like this conversation. It was awkward and embarrassing to be put in the position of expert on dieting. She hadn't been on a diet in her life. What did she know?

'I want to lose twenty pounds,' Josie said with the zeal of the newly converted. She was still staring at her toes, but her eyes were focussed on some inner vision of her new self, Lauren could tell.

'That's too much! You'll look like death warmed over!'

Josie sighed longingly. 'Wouldn't it be great?'

Steve came sauntering over. 'Have you deserted me?' he asked Josie.

'I just wanted to tell Lauren how much I enjoyed her party last night. I'm going to lose twenty pounds,' she added in the same breath. 'Don't you think I'll look great?'

Steve put his freckled arm around her. 'You know who my favourite painter is,' he stated, winking at her.

Rubens, no doubt.

He smiled lovingly at Josie. 'I like you just the way you are.'

Thousands of men said that to their wives and didn't mean it. Steve did. He adored Josie. She could have sprouted horns and a tail and he'd still love her. Josie was one of the few genuinely happy people Lauren knew. Loving kindness radiated from her. Her eyes were always laughing, her mouth always smiling. She was ready day and night to do anything for anybody. Plain Josie had a beauty no money could buy and no cosmetic could create. And as Lauren sat there, watching the two of them smiling at each other, she felt envy seep into her every pore. At that moment she would have cheerfully given up her good looks for just a piece of their happiness.

Her eyes drifted towards Joel. He seemed very relaxed and his eyes were closed. Had he fallen asleep? But no, a moment later he swung himself into a sitting position and leaned his forearms on his knees. He began to talk with Steve and Lauren got up to take another swim. She felt unaccountably depressed.

When she got back to her lounger, Josie was describing the marvels of a restaurant in Chinatown. It was just a little place tucked away in some cat-ridden alley with Formica tables and flies and not-too-clean cutlery, she said, but the food was straight from heaven. She plunged into an enthusiastic and detailed description of the dishes she and Steve had sampled there the week before.

One thing led to another. Steve invited Joel and Lauren to join them for dinner at the Chinese restaurant that evening.

It was impossible to refuse. Not that she wanted to, of course. For a moment big containers of food left over from last night's party floated before her eyes. It would take a week for her to eat it all. Most of it would probably perish in the refrigerator. She'd tell Yanti and her sister to please take it home.

For a moment she was afraid that Joel might decline the invitation, but he did not. Well, it was Sunday, wasn't it? She was happy to spend the evening with some friends. Maybe he was too.

'We'll come and pick you up at seven,' decided Josie. 'It's easier to go in one car. That way you won't get lost trying to follow us around in all those little alleys.'

Fatigue was making itself felt. Lauren could barely move. Her body felt like rubber. Her head was beginning to ache from the heat. Several hours in the glaring sun after only a few hours of sleep had done her in. She went home.

In her absence the house had undergone a metamorphosis. It looked its old bare self again, except for the flowers still sitting uncomplaining in their tin cans and glass jars. The furniture had been put back where it belonged. The floors shone with cleanliness. The kitchen sparkled. All the borrowed dishes and glasses had been washed and were ready for distribution to their various owners, and the place smelled like a hospital.

Lauren paid the girls double rate for working overtime and begged them to unburden her of the left-over food that was overloading the refrigerator.

Too tired to eat anything, she arranged her weary limbs on the bed and sank into the merciful oblivion of sleep. When she finally drifted back into consciousness it was late. She hurried through the shower to get rid of the cobwebs in her brain while she agonised over what to wear. Nothing very dressy, of course. She pulled on lightweight white slacks and a black, sleeveless tunic and belted it with a long silk scarf from India. She let her hair hang loose and put on make-up in record time. When the doorbell rang she was ready.

They wound their way through the narrow alleys of Chinatown, which looked picturesque in the sparse light of an occasional bulb or pressure lamp. Joel was sitting next to Lauren in the back seat, cool as could be, while she was shivering inside like a fool because of his nearness.

She tried to concentrate on the sights outside, noting the architecture of the small houses with their overhanging second floors and their green and blue painted doors. In these narrow streets not many cars ventured, but the *becaks* were everywhere—bicycle taxis carrying passengers on benches built in front of the steering bar. Young men spent their days wheeling their customers all over town, and their legs were iron-hard masses of muscle. Sometimes, when a hill was too steep, Lauren would see the driver push the *becak* rather than ride it. It would always amaze her that the passengers would stay in their seat, sitting comfortably, while the poor guy would struggle and strain to push them up the hill.

The restaurant was just as Josie had described it, singularly unimpressive. It was obviously a neighbour-hood eating place, not meant for fancy foreigners. Six or seven tables filled the small room. Fluorescent lights glared down on Formica table tops and bare terrazzo floor tiles. A tomato-red television set showed a German cartoon and a variety of clocks and calendars decorated the walls. In the corner a motorcycle was stored under a murky blue plastic cover.

Joel pulled out a chair for her and she sat down. He took the chair next to hers. They ordered beer and soft drinks. The warm air was filled with delicious cooking smells. An air-conditioning unit in the wall hummed bravely and ineffectually and a tired fan moved slowly.

At another table a Chinese family were having their evening meal. The little boy gazed at them with solemn eyes, his chopsticks idle in his hand.

Bottles and glasses were placed in front of them by a young man in jeans and shirt unbuttoned halfway down his chest. A gold chain encircled his brown neck. They studied the menu, which was written in both Chinese and Indonesian.

'The frogs' legs are good,' said Josie. 'Taste just like chicken.'

'And the corn and crab soup,' added Steve. 'What do you like, Lauren?'

'Everything. You order, I'll eat.'

'Same here,' added Joel. He was leaning back in his chair, looking very relaxed. He grinned at Josie. 'I have great confidence in your taste.' Josie flushed a little and seemed pleased to take charge.

There followed a true repast—corn and crab soup, fried frogs' legs, beef with vegetables and ginger, a large fish complete with head and tail in a delicious sweet red sauce, mounds of steaming white rice.

They were given red and black lacquered chopsticks and plates with gaudy red roses and sparkling white, starched napkins.

They ate and talked. Joel amused them with stories of his various stays in Malaysia and Japan, and Josie was totally enthralled. The food was truly delicious, Joel was truly charming, and Josie was truly enchanted. She was falling for him hook, line and sinker, but in a totally innocent way. The only man she would ever go home with was her own Steve. In her imagination, Lauren could hear her talk about Joel after they arrived home tonight. Wasn't he handsome? Smart? Charming? Exciting? Why wouldn't an interesting man like him be married? Did Steve think he was divorced? Lauren could imagine Steve's answer: 'He isn't married because he's waiting for somebody like you.' She could hear Josie's delighted laughter.

She examined the calendars on the wall. One had a picture of a woman slinkily draped over the hood of a shiny car. Another featured a bottle of beer. There were seven calendars in all. She counted three clocks and a barometer, three mirrors, and seven electric fans of which only one was actually working. The others were rusty and silent and stared sulkily at the customers from their various locations in the room. She counted the tables. Seven. She looked up at the ceiling. Seven lights.

Looking down again, she noticed Joel staring at her, eyebrows raised.

'What are you doing?' he queried.

'Taking inventory.'

'I see.' His tone carried a wealth of meaning.

'There are seven fans in this place,' she said. 'And seven calendars and seven tables and seven lights in the ceiling.'

Joel, Steve and Josie looked around the room, counting.

'You're right,' announced Steve.

'I'm real good at counting,' Lauren said, grinning.

'Do you think it means something?' Josie asked.

Joel nodded. 'It's called coincidence.'

'Oh.' Josie looked disappointed.

He gave her a charming smile. 'Or seven could just be the owner's lucky number.'

Josie's face brightened. 'Yes! I've heard of that sort of thing!'

Lauren sipped her tea from the little round cup, wishing she were somewhere else instead of here in a Chinese restaurant making inane conversation about the number of fans and calendars on the wall. Joel was being so charming to Josie. Why wasn't he paying more attention to her? He was sitting two feet away from her and the temptation to touch him was unbearable. The air between them was electric, like it always was, and although no outward signs showed on his face, Joel was aware of it.

Why didn't he smile at her the way he smiled at Josie? Why was he always slightly reticent with her? What was it that kept him from acknowledging that there was something between them—something vital and alive? He had kissed her the night of the party, but it had seemed strangely unreal and even now she wasn't sure if it had really happened. But she remembered the feelings and the highly charged atmosphere, and she clutched at the memory, the feeling of safety and belonging. She wanted to close her eyes and drift back into it.

She became aware of a silence, and glanced around the table. All three of them were staring at her.

'What are you thinking about, Lauren?' asked Joel, scrutinising her face. 'Never mind,' he added, 'thoughts are private. I shouldn't ask.'

The food dropped from between her chopsticks. She had the most peculiar feeling that he was looking straight into her mind.

'Nothing much,' she said lightly, attempting a smile. She gathered up another mouthful of food and brought it carefully towards her mouth. Josie was still looking at her. She was wondering if she'd fallen in love with Joel. Josie would like to be a witness to a developing romance. Lauren would love to be a participant in a romance.

'Not nothing much,' stated Josie, 'but if it's a dark secret, please don't tell us.' Steve seemed oblivious to the conversation. He was concentrating on the extraction of the last bits of meat from the bones of the fish swimming in the red sauce. The colour reminded Lauren of the bright orange-red flowers of her green bean tree.

'Actually,' she said, suddenly inspired, 'I was

thinking about my green bean tree.' If she didn't say something Josie wouldn't leave it alone.

'What about it?'

'It's blooming—orangey-red flowers, very pretty. And all the pods are brown and shrivelled up.'

Joel regarded her with eyebrows raised. 'What, pray, is a green bean tree?'

'I don't know,' she said truthfully. 'It's a tree in the back of my house.' She described the tree, saying she'd noticed a lot of the same trees all over town. 'I keep telling myself to ask somebody what kind of tree it is, but I keep forgetting. So, for want of a better name, I call it my green bean tree. I look at it every morning when I sit on the verandah with my cup of tea.'

He nodded his understanding. 'And now your green bean tree is blooming.' He was making fun of her, she could tell by the silvery glint of amusement in his eyes, but she didn't mind.

'Only on a few branches. Maybe because it's been so dry.'

'You could try talking to it,' he suggested, straight-faced. 'While you're having your tea.'

'It's a thought,' she said, equally straight-faced.

'And if that fails,' added Steve, 'you could play it some music. Mozart or Beethoven should do.'

Josie giggled. Lauren nodded thoughtfully. 'I have a little portable cassette player I can take out on the verandah with me. I suppose I'd have to turn it up loud. It might bother the neighbours.' She doubted whether Joel or her neighbours on the other side would be able to hear anything.

'As long as it's either Mozart or Beethoven I have no objections,' said Joel amiably. 'But Vivaldi is best, if you ask me. Just don't make it punk rock or the tree will die for sure and I'll make serious objections.'

Lauren wondered what he would do to make her stop.

'The easiest thing to do,' she said, 'is to tell the
gardener to water it more often.'

Joel nodded. 'I wondered if anyone would come up
with that suggestion.' Then he smiled at her and her
heart leaped. He leaned a little closer. 'And your green
bean tree is called a poinciana. A couple of more
weeks and the whole town will be dressed in red. It'll be
quite a sight.'

After they left the restaurant they discovered in one
of the dim streets the lights of a Chinese temple. It was
quite nearby, but they had not noticed it before.

'You think we could go in?' whispered Josie.

The doors were wide open, guarded by massive stone
temple dogs. Lauren's first impressions were those of
masses of burning red candles and the overwhelming
fragrance of incense.

Joel said it was all right to go in; he'd been there
before and visitors were welcome.

Quietly they entered, looking around in awe. The
colours red and black and gold dominated the interior.
Large red silk lanterns decorated with black and gold
paintings hung from the high ceiling. Enormous brass
bowls held countless sticks of burning incense. Shrines
skirted the large central area, each featuring an
elaborately painted statue of Confucius, or a gold
Buddha, or some other saintly-looking Chinese in
ornate dress. Lauren examined the different shrines.
Each was individually decorated with gold carved
dragons, silk lanterns, gold and red banners, shiny brass
bowls of incense, burning candles and exotic paintings.
Here and there she noticed small bunches of fresh
flowers and tiny cups of tea set out to welcome visitors.

The temple was permeated with the mystery of the
Orient, and unconsciously they were whispering to each
other as they moved around.

Outside again they noticed the Chinese garden across
from the temple entrance. Someone opened the gate

and invited them in to have a look. They entered a different world. It was a garden straight out of a Chinese painting, exquisitely planned and laid out with rock formations and lovely plants and flowers and benches to sit on.

Lauren wandered off by herself. She wanted to be alone.

There was an absolute stillness, an absence of time and motion. Not a breeze stirred the leaves. In the endless darkness above were the countless stars and a full moon, throwing shadows, dark and still, around the garden. She sat down on a stone bench and put her hands in her lap.

Those same stars, that same moon had belonged to different nights in different places and she had looked at them so many times, feeling small and insignificant compared to the awesomeness of their eternity. She had a curious sense of weightlessness, as if she could no longer feel her body. It rose in her again, the familiar mood of melancholy sadness, the longing for something she couldn't have.

A large shape loomed over her. Joel. She felt a sudden fierce pain. Her eyes filled with tears and her hands, without her wanting them to, reached out to him.

'Lauren? Are you ready to go?'

The words broke the spell, and her arms fell by her sides.

He came a step closer, looking at her quizzically. 'Is something wrong?'

She shook her head, turning her face away from him. She didn't trust herself to speak.

'Lauren,' he said softly, 'why are you crying?'

'I don't know.' Her voice was thick. 'It's nothing.' She stood up hastily and as she did she caught a glimpse of his face. Maybe the shadows of this mysterious garden distorted reality, for certainly in this still and peaceful place nothing seemed quite real. It seemed that for a fleeting moment she saw pain in his face.

Quickly she stepped past him and moved to the gate. He didn't follow her, for when she glanced back he was still standing where she had left him. In the solitude of the garden with the pale moonlight washing over him, he seemed to her lonely and forlorn. Sadness overwhelmed her as she watched him, and then he looked in her direction as if he had felt her gaze or her thoughts. Slowly he came down the path towards her. The gate was locked behind them and without a word they walked into the street.

They found the car with Josie and Steve already in it, and slid into the back seat. They were all strangely subdued as they drove home through the narrow streets of Chinatown. A few children were still up, playing hopscotch, and here and there Lauren noticed men asleep on mats or benches in front of their houses. A large rat scooted across an alley and slipped away under a wall.

Reality—what was that?

Lauren kept hoping that Joel would invite her for lunch or dinner or drinks, but the weeks passed and he did not. They kept meeting in various places, unplanned, always, and slowly the tension between them built. It was there, undeniable, even though there were no outward signs of it.

Their conversations seemed quite relaxed, but they never discussed anything more intimate than politics, the drought problems and Indonesian culture. On one level they were nothing more than casual acquaintances and neighbours. Joel kept his distance, a wall of reserve Lauren dared not break through.

On another level she felt she had known him all her life. She kept feeling the vibrations between them, breaking through the reserves, yet they never acknowledged their existence in words. She kept having the mysterious feeling that they were connected by invisible threads of thought and feeling and memory. She began to wonder if it really were coincidence that they kept meeting.

These thoughts were passing through her mind one night as she was sipping a drink at a gathering at a friend's house. She couldn't get into the party spirit. She felt brittle, as if the slightest breeze would make her disintegrate into a heap of rubble on the floor. Why was nothing happening? What was it that kept the two of them apart? Dispirited, she gazed into her empty glass. She couldn't sit here all night being miserable. With a sigh she unwound herself from the chair and replaced her glass on the table. Taking a handful of cashew nuts from a bowl, she wandered outside into the sultry night. Joel was there, talking to some people, one of them Anne Furgeson. She was always hovering around him. Like a fly, Lauren thought nastily. A blue and green and purple fly.

Sten was there too, with his pretty blonde wife. Ever since she had returned to Indonesia he had lost interest in Lauren, for which she thanked the gods. All that passed between them now was a casual hello-how-are-you.

She sauntered over to the little group and joined them.

'When are you leaving?' asked Anne.

'In two weeks,' said Joel.

Lauren didn't know he'd been planning a trip. 'Where are you going?' she asked, feeling a sudden sense of doom.

'To the States. I'll be back in three weeks.'

Anne turned to Lauren. Her face, made up to perfection, seemed quite expressionless, but her eyes held a gleam of malice. 'He just told us he's going home to get married.'

CHAPTER FOUR

LAUREN didn't know exactly how it happened, but the next moment she was choking, gasping for breath. No air. Something was lodged in her throat and she couldn't breathe. *She could not breathe!*

Terror seized her. She was dying. She grasped her throat. Not a sound came out. Faces stared at her, horrified, frozen. She couldn't breathe and she couldn't speak and she couldn't even ask for help. This is it, she thought, I'm going to choke to death on a cashew nut while people are staring at me, doing nothing. What a way to go!

Somebody moved—Joel. In a flash he was behind her, arms around her, fist on her sternum, slamming it into her. The cashew nut flew out, like a projectile, landing somewhere in the rose bushes.

Air flowed back into her in ragged spurts. Her chest hurt. Tears streamed down her cheeks, and faces and plants and furniture swirled around. Her legs gave out. Joel caught her and lifted her up in his arms, and her head sagged on his shoulder. She had no strength at all. Her muscles had melted away into nothing. He carried her away and put her down on a bed somewhere. He took off her glasses. Everything was blurred and she was shaking so hard her teeth were chattering.

'You're all right now,' he said soothingly.

Somebody entered the room with a drink and Joel held the glass to her lips, one arm around her shoulders for support. 'It's just water,' he said. 'Try and drink it slowly.'

She couldn't have done anything else. Her teeth clinked against the glass. After a few sips she pushed the glass away and covered her face with her hands. She was sobbing now. Her body shook and tears ran through her fingers. She was too shaken to care that he was seeing her like this.

He put his arms around her and held her against him. For a moment the comfort of his body so close to hers was like a balm to her frazzled nerves.

But only for a moment.

She felt a surge of bitter anger. I have to practically *die* before he'd touch me! she thought wildly. She hated him then. She hated him for not loving her, for marrying someone else, for a thousand unknown reasons. She sobbed in his arms like a helpless child.

'It's all right now, it's over,' he said gently.

It's not all right! she wanted to shout. How can you do this to me? How can you marry somebody else and bring her back here to live right next door? She wanted to shout out her anger and beat his chest with her fists, but she lay in his arms, weak and limp and unmoving.

The truth hammered in her brain. He loved another woman. He didn't love her. He would never love her. He was going to marry someone else. Oh, God, she couldn't stand it. It was like a nightmare and it wouldn't end, would never end. Joel didn't love her and all her secret hopes and illusions lay shattered at her feet like jagged bits of glass.

She clung to him. She loved him and she hated him, and she had never been so miserable in all her life.

She would have to calm down. She could not let herself become hysterical. She *had* to compose herself. She stopped crying, taking a deep, shuddering breath, then slowly she quieted down. She felt empty.

Joel released her after a while and handed her the glass of water. She drank it all. There was a box of tissues on the bedside table, and she blew her nose and wiped her eyes. Then she picked up her glasses and put them back on. Everything seemed clear and well defined. Everything *was* clear and well defined.

'I'm sorry I made such a scene,' she said, looking down on her wrinkled dress. Her face felt puffed and swollen and she must look like something out of a horror movie.

'You're forgiven,' he said, smiling. 'Teetering on the edge of death probably isn't a positive experience.'

If only that had been all!

Lauren struggled for self-control and a measure of detachment. 'I don't recommend it.' It sounded beautifully cool.

'You scared the hell out of us all,' Joel told her.

'I was a bit disturbed myself! I wasn't quite ready to bail out yet. I have a few plans for the future.'

'Such as what?' His tone was light.

'I haven't been to Bali yet.'

'I see what you mean.'

'And I want to go down the Columbia river on a raft.'

'That's pretty risky.'

'So is chewing cashew nuts.'

He laughed. 'You have a point there!'

Lauren smoothed the wrinkles in her dress. She was sitting cross-legged on the bed, her hair falling down around her face, looking and feeling awful. She gazed at the bedspread, which was a vivid tomato-red. Her dress was a deep burgundy and the two colours clashed horribly. They were in a spare bedroom, it seemed, because it looked bare and unused. Joel got off the bed and sat down on the only available chair, and she raised her eyes, seeing him clearly for the first time since they had entered the room.

A lock of hair hung over his forehead. He seemed a little pale, but that could be her imagination. It could be the glaring fluorescent light. His eyes seemed darker than usual.

Her heart contracted in a spasm of pain. She loved him. Would she ever stop loving him? Forget him? She steeled herself and took a deep mental breath.

'What's her name—the girl you're going to marry?'

'Sharon.' No inflection in his voice.

'Do you love her?' She was surprised at her audacity. Asking a question like that was not exactly the epitome of discretion.

His expression did not change. 'Yes.'

Lauren let that sink in, digesting it cold-bloodedly. She might as well start right away to face the facts. Joel loved Sharon. Joel was going to marry Sharon. She, Lauren, loved Joel, which was too bad. Better luck next time.

'Tell me about her.'

'I'd prefer not to.' His voice was calm and quiet.

'Why not? I'll get to meet her when you get back, won't I?'

'Yes.' He shrugged. 'All right, if you insist. What do you want to know?'

'How old is she? What does she look like? What does she do?'

His face was impassive. 'She's twenty-five. She has blue eyes and fair hair and she's five foot four. She's a high school maths teacher. She's divorced and has two-year-old twin boys.' He was reciting the facts without emotion. He had come to his feet while he was talking and his back was turned to her. She couldn't see his face.

Lauren said nothing.

'And in case you're wondering,' he continued in the same level tone, 'her husband left her when she was eight months pregnant. The bastard took their only car and all their savings.'

Oh, God, Lauren thought, a sob story! It made her angry, she didn't know why. Did he want her to feel sorry for Sharon? She tried to imagine what it would be like to be pregnant and deserted, to be left without a cent. It wasn't an experience she cared to have. Had Joel come to Sharon's rescue? Had he dragged her up out of her pit of misery?

What did she care?

Why was she so angry?

She had her own private pit of misery and it seemed she'd have to climb out of it unaided. No Prince Charming for her. Joel was galloping away with another woman on his horse, leaving her right where she was.

She closed her eyes. She didn't want to think about him and that other woman. She'd asked for the information in a fit of bravery, but she couldn't take any more. Later she'd think about it again. All she wanted now was oblivion—sleep. For a year.

She uncurled her legs and got off the bed. Joel turned and came towards her, his face calm and composed.

'Shall I take you home?'

She shook her head. 'I'm all right, I can go myself.' Her voice was dull. She wasn't as steady as she'd thought. Her legs were still trembling and shakily she walked over to the door. He took her hand as if she were a child.

'I'll take you.' There was quiet determination in his tone and she had no strength to resist. After all, was it a sin to lean on a strong man who had just torn you from the clutches of death?

Oh, Joel, she said silently, why is this happening to us? Why are you doing this? Tell me it's all a mistake. Tell me you love me.

But he didn't say any of these things. He asked for her car keys instead. She handed them to him.

'What about your car?' she asked. 'How are you going to get it home?' She didn't really care, but it was something to say, something to normalise her thought pattern.

'I'll go running in the morning and pick it up.' He helped her into the Toyota as if she were an invalid. Then he got behind the wheel and started the engine. They drove home in strained silence. Joel parked the car in the garage and handed her back the keys. They stood in front of her door and she knew she would have to thank him, tell him how grateful she was that he had saved her life. The trouble was that she didn't feel very grateful.

'Thank you,' she said. 'You saved my life.' It sounded theatrical and insincere, as if she was reciting a line in an amateur high school play.

Joel laughed softly. 'Let's not be too dramatic about it. It was my pleasure. Goodnight, Lauren, sleep well.'

'Goodnight.'

She wanted to break down in tears all over again.

He turned and strode off into the dark, out of her life.

Opening the door, she went in, closing it without looking back. Like a zombie she trudged into the bedroom, took off her clothes, dropping them in a heap on a chair, and fell into bed. This evening she had come close to death, but she was still alive. Joel had saved her life.

The terrible thing was that she didn't even care. There didn't seem anything worth living for.

She slept. At twenty to six she surfaced from a light, restless sleep and realised that it was Sunday. She stumbled out of bed and into the bathroom. Two black eyes gazed dully back at her from the mirror. Last night she had disobeyed the holiest command of beauty care: Thou Shalt Not Retire at Night Without Removing All Make-Up and Thoroughly Cleansing Thy Face. She wondered what punishment was awaiting her. Instant wrinkles? Pimples? Dry skin? The Heartbreak of Psoriasis? She cleaned her face and peered into the mirror. Everything looked just fine. Maybe any moment now Helena Rubinstein would appear in front of her, wagging her finger. 'Naughty, naughty,' she'd say. 'We'll give you one more chance.'

She made a pot of tea and sat on her bedroom verandah and examined the green bean tree. In the last week it had broken into full, blazing bloom, the vibrancy of the orange colour almost artificial in its intensity.

Everything was peaceful and quiet. She should have gone jogging this morning, but she didn't have the energy. A large butterfly, brown, black and white, fluttered around the hibiscus bush, then changed its mind and disappeared around the corner of the house. The tea was hot and she burned her tongue. The muezzin began his call to worship, his chant a wail wafting over the neighbourhood.

She felt numb.

For almost an hour she just sat there, staring at the sky and the trees and the flowers and the people walking down the road. Then she crawled back into bed. She had nothing better to do. It was cool in the bedroom and she fell asleep, not waking up again until almost eleven. She made coffee, put her briefcase open on the big bed and took out a stack of survey forms. They had been taken to several villages by university students who had asked the people the questions and filled them out.

Here, reduced to a few statements and numbers, were the lives of village women—the age at which they had married, the number of children they had, their source of income, specific information about their jobs and a time schedule of their daily activities.

The answers varied little. They had all been married at an early age, had four or five children, and derived their income from cottage industries such as batik waxing, tofu making, bean sprouting, basket weaving, pottery making or sewing.

There were no questions about the emotional state of their lives—Are you happy? Do you love your husband? Are you content with your lot? Are you fulfilled in your work? At this particular moment Lauren would have found the answers to those questions far more interesting.

She was hungry. In the kitchen she loaded a tray with cheese, crackers, a banana, some peanuts and a glass of iced tea. On second thoughts she put the peanuts back in the cupboard. They reminded her of cashew nuts.

Sitting cross-legged on the bed, she resumed her reading, eating as she went along. It was one o'clock and she still hadn't dressed. As it turned out, she didn't dress the entire day. There seemed to be no point to it. She spent the time reading on the bed and eating on the bed and just sitting on the bed and staring at the bare wall. She should go jogging now, but she still didn't feel up to it. The Community Centre had organised a spaghetti dinner in the afternoon. She didn't go. The telephone rang twice and she let it ring. She'd never done that in her life. You could never tell what great surprise or wonderful news you'd miss if you did. For dinner she ate more cheese and crackers.

A noise woke her up in the middle of the night. Lying still, listening, she tried to identify it. It sounded as if someone was shovelling gravel—strange at this hour of the night. Lauren glanced at the clock. It was three forty-two. Struggling out of bed, she moved over to the window and peered out into the night. By the side of the road that led past the *kampong* below her house stood a truck with a load of gravel, and two men were shovelling it out by the spadeful. A few street lamps illuminated the area and the trees threw warped shadows over the scene. It looked spooky.

Roadworks in the middle of the night! Lauren groaned as she crawled back under the sheet. Well, it was safer and cooler, she had to admit that. The day started early here.

Not even the hum of the refrigerator drowned out the sounds coming from outside. Sleep eluded her and she lay awake for the rest of the night, cursing the gravel shovellers and aware of an increasing number of sounds as the morning dawned—roosters and chickens and dogs and the gongs and bells of food vendors peddling their wares.

At five-thirty she put on shorts, a shirt and running shoes and went jogging. She had to force herself. It might refresh her body if not her spirit. She was in terrible shape after only a few hours of sleep, and when she came back she felt worse.

She went to the office early and started her working day with another fight with Ed. One of his outrageous male chauvinist remarks sent her off into a wild fury. He stared at her open-mouthed as she unleashed on him her wrath, giving him her opinion of his sexist, biased, bigoted, overbearing, narrowminded, prejudiced, discriminating and arrogant ideas about women. She was truly explosive and amazingly eloquent, and it felt wonderful to spew her fury without restraint. Ed kept staring at her even after she'd stopped because she'd run out of words. He had never seen her like that.

Lauren had never seen herself like that, either. Turning on her heel, she marched to her desk and plonked herself down on the chair and stared at the wall to cool off. A collage of charts and graphs and notices and maps and a Garfield poster stared back at her. She looked down at her desk. In front of her was a report on leadership training. She was supposed to read it. She read it. The office was deadly quiet. On the other side of the room Ed sat at his desk, working. He hadn't said a single word to her for an hour. He was probably writing a lengthy letter to the desk officer in Jakarta this very minute, reporting her insubordination.

Lauren didn't care.

Ten minutes later the silence was broken by the sound of his chair scraping over the terrazzo. She heard him get up.

'Would you like a cup of coffee?' he asked in a perfectly normal voice.

'Please.' She kept her gaze down on the report, busily making notes in the margins with light pencil marks.

'I'll be right back.'

Fifteen minutes later he returned, put a cup of coffee in front of her and a plate with a doughnut on it. He must have gone to the Danish Bakery to get it. Was it a peace-offering? He perched himself casually on the corner of her desk in an effort to look cool.

'Now,' he said, 'why don't you tell me what's really bugging you?'

Lauren couldn't believe her ears.

'Thanks for the coffee and the doughnut,' she said evasively.

'You've been acting funny lately. What gives, kid?'

'You're imagining things. I had a bad night, that's all. I apologise for losing my temper. I shouldn't have let myself go like that. I'm sorry.'

'Forget it. I have the skin of an elephant.'

'And the tolerance,' she added, giving a half-smile.

Ed grinned back at her. 'You're not so bad, kid.'

Lauren wished he'd stop calling her kid. It was one of the things that irritated her no end. She was an adult, an independent person, a professional. And he called her kid! To him, with his fifty-odd years, she was a mere babe, but it wasn't very businesslike to show it. She had the distinct impression that he didn't quite take her seriously. It seemed to her that he was inwardly smiling at her benevolently, goodhumouredly letting her play her games, indulging her. Had he no idea how funny he looked trying to act cool and macho while he gave himself away half the time acting like a grandpa?

Ed cleared his throat and got up from Lauren's desk. He stood next to her chair, hesitating, and she wondered what was next. He didn't look at her. 'I'm not as terrible as all that, am I?'

She didn't ask for clarification. It was clear what he meant. She wanted to say that yes, he really was as bad as all that, but she took pity on him.

'Of course not. Only a little.' After all, he'd let her off the hook, so the least she could do was show him her charity. His ego had enough problems as it was. She took a bite from the doughnut. 'This is really good,' she said. 'Thanks again.'

He grinned a little sheepishly. 'You're welcome.'

They went back to work.

Yanti had packed her a lunch and she ate it at her desk while she worked on a visual aid chart for one of her training programmes. She used pictures rather than words since many older women couldn't read or write, and often spoke only Javanese. She drew little stick figures in bright colours with round faces and bright smiles or sad expressions. It was fun to do. It made her feel as if she were back in nursery school, drawing pretty pictures of houses and trees and flowers.

Ed was entertaining a consultant from the States and she had the office to herself. He had asked her to join them for lunch, but she had declined.

It was Monday, but she didn't go to the Hash that afternoon. Time dragged. She read. She ate. She took a long bath and went to bed.

The days went by in a blur. Ed asked her why she was so quiet and she said it was to make up for her outburst on Monday. He decided she needed a trip; she'd been in the office too long. Fine, she said, whatever you like. He gave her an odd look and she ignored it.

She felt like a swimmer seeing no shore. She waded through the days feeling increasingly dull, dumb and dead. It took an effort to get out of bed in the morning. Breakfast has lost all its appeal. She felt incapable of thinking a straight thought.

On Thursday night she was sitting on the verandah

with her *kopi tubruk*, staring dully at the moon, when she heard footsteps coming down the driveway, and her heart began to pound. The driveway was hidden from view by a couple of huge cactuses and she couldn't see who was coming to the door. But there was no need to see; she knew.

A minute later Joel stepped on to the verandah, wearing white shorts, a dark shirt and sandals, and oozing vigour and vitality.

'Hi,' he said, 'Yanti told me where to find you.'

'Hi. Have a seat.'

He sat down. 'Nice place,' he commented, looking at the plants and the trees around the verandah. 'Is that your green bean tree?'

Lauren nodded. 'It's blooming like crazy now.'

'Who did it? Mozart, Beethoven, or Vivaldi?'

She grinned and pointed to the sky. 'I think it was Allah. I didn't do a thing.'

'You can't beat celestial help,' he stated. 'That colour is quite spectacular, isn't it?'

'Yes. Would you like a cup of coffee?' She felt awkward and nervous and she wished she was wearing something a little more substantial than a length of batik cloth tied under her arms.

'Yes, please.'

She jumped to her feet, glad to have something to do, but before she had a chance, Yanti appeared with a cup in her hand.

'*Terima kasih*,' she said, taking it from Yanti and sitting down again. The enamel pot was on the table in front of her and she poured carefully so as not to disturb the grounds on the bottom.

'Sugar? Milk?' Her hand was shaking. *Good God*, she said to herself, *calm down*!

'Just black, please.'

She handed him his cup. 'Here you go. Hope it's not too strong.'

'Thanks. It's never too strong for me.'

Lauren wondered how long they were going to go on with this polite little chit chat. It was getting on her nerves.

'I haven't seen you for a while,' Joel said casually, taking a drink from his coffee. 'I thought I'd check up on you to see if you're all right.'

She was definitely not all right.

'I'm fine,' she lied. His concern surprised her. He had never come to her house before, unannounced, uninvited. 'I only wish we'd get some rain and a little relief from the wretched heat,' she added for good measure.

'They say the rains will be late this year. It doesn't look very good. Everything is terribly dry.'

Oh, God, she thought, I can't stand this. She shifted restlessly in her chair, not knowing what to do with her arms and legs. 'The humidity is what makes it so unbearable. Yesterday there were all those clouds and not a drop of rain. I hate it! I spend half my time in my bedroom with the air-conditioning on. I feel like a prisoner in that bare little room.'

There was a silence while they drank their coffee. Down below by the road a food vendor had installed himself with his little two-wheeled cart and was ringing his bell to call attention to his presence. A dog barked. A Yamaha roared by.

Joel put his cup down and she glanced at him quickly. 'Are you getting the house ready for your wife?'

A slight pause. 'I think I'm pretty well organised. The place was painted before I moved in and they fixed up the kitchen a little with some more cabinets and a couple of shelves.'

'What about servants? Will you need someone for the children?'

'I thought I'd leave it to Sharon when she comes.'

Lauren trailed a finger around the rim of her cup,

following the movement with her eyes. 'Yanti has a younger sister, seventeen, who used to work for a German family with three children. She's not working at the moment. Just say the word and she'll be over to talk to you.' Cool and calm. She was doing well.

'Thanks, I'll keep it in mind.'

'Has she . . . Sharon . . . ever been overseas?'

He shook his head. 'No. It will be quite an adjustment for her. I think she'll like it here, though.'

'Maybe she'll be able to find work at the school—the International School, I mean. They're always looking for qualified teachers.'

Joel stretched his legs out and the chair creaked. 'Actually, she's looking forward to not working for a while. She wants to spend some time with the boys while they're still small. It was impossible to stay home with them before. She didn't have a cent and she had to support them.'

'What about the father?' she asked. 'Didn't he at least pay child support?'

Somebody else was having this conversation. It wasn't her, it couldn't possibly be her.

Joel's eyes were hard. 'The bastard disappeared into the blue yonder. She's never had a cent from him, and they can't find him to make him pay up.' His voice was hard and cold. The only time Lauren had ever noticed strong emotion in him was when he talked about Sharon. Well, he loved her, didn't he?

She poured more coffee. 'You'll have an instant family,' she said casually. 'Do you like the idea?'

He smiled. It warmed his face and lit up his eyes. 'It doesn't sound half bad to me to be the father of two sons. At my age it's about time to have some. And those two boys are bright little kids. Lots of spark, like their mother.'

Why didn't she feel any pain? She felt numb, anaesthetised. Somehow this wasn't real, or maybe her mind was refusing to acknowledge it out of self-defence.

Lots of spark, like their mother. Somehow, Lauren's mental picture of Sharon as a weeping willow could not easily incorporate the fact that she had spark. And if she wanted to be brave and take a critical look at herself, Lauren had to admit that when it came to sparks, she wasn't exactly setting the world on fire these days with her vivacious and exuberant spirit. This past week she had practically buried herself in the bedroom, isolating herself from everybody and everything. Who was she to pass judgment?

At my age, he'd said. He was thirty-six, he'd told her once. Most men had children by then. Many men by then were married for the second time and raising other men's children, while their own were being brought up by the mother alone or together with a stepfather.

'You have no children, then?' she asked. 'You haven't been married before?'

'No.' The left corner of his mouth curled up and his eyes were amused. She didn't know what was so funny.

'Why not?'

He shrugged. 'I never wanted to. And you?'

'No one ever asked me. They're all scared of me.'

He threw back his head and laughed out loud. It was a wonderful sound, deep and rich, and she hadn't heard it very often. Lauren couldn't help smiling. For a moment he studied her intently.

'Actually,' he said thoughtfully, 'I think you could very well be right. You're smarter than most; you probably intimidate the hell out of them.'

There was some truth in that, but she certainly didn't intimidate Joel. Maybe that was one of the reasons she was drawn to him.

'That's the burden of the modern career woman,' she said melodramatically. 'You read about it all the time. We suffer a lot for using our brains. All the men scurry off into dark corners at the sight of us. And the ones that don't are already snatched up.'

He grinned. 'This is a very dangerous conversation.'

'Let's change the topic.'

'What would you like to talk about?'

'Drink. You want one?'

'Why not? The night is young.'

Wrong, she thought. All wrong. What she didn't need now was for him to stay here with her under the stars and the moon with palms whispering seductively in the breeze. One drink and her inhibitions and her common sense might melt away into nothingness and who could tell what might happen? Something might snap. Maybe she'd start yelling at him, as she'd done to Ed, or worse, fall all over him.

She considered telling him she was out of everything. No Scotch, no gin, no vodka. Being a smart man, he'd no doubt get the message. Another option was to give him a drink and have soda water herself.

She came to her feet, tying the *kain* a little more securely. 'What would you like?'

'Scotch on the rocks, please.' Joel raised himself out of the creaky chair and followed her in to the bar, which was built in the corner of the living room. It was the first house or apartment she had lived in overseas that had a built-in bar. Stocking it up had made her feel downright decadent. Apart from her Campari, a bottle of Scotch and gin, she had never had anything around. Now she had an impressive array of bottles, most of which she never touched herself. It was nice to be able to offer your guests a choice, and besides, you couldn't very well have an empty bar in your house, right?

For the rest the house was quite modest—nothing ostentatious about it. The kitchen was a miracle of inconvenience and the bathroom needed re-tiling rather desperately. But she'd seen a lot worse on her travels. Single, short-term people took what they could get.

Leaning a hip against the side of the bar, Joel watched her as she fixed his drink. He made her nervous and her hands shook. She promptly dropped an ice cube and it slithered away across the floor. They bent over at the same time to retrieve it. They didn't bump heads, but they came close. He picked up the ice cube and dropped it in an empty ashtray.

Their eyes met and Lauren looked away.

'I'm making you nervous,' he said. 'Why is that?'

'I'll ask my analyst.' She forced a smile and put the drink in front of him on the bar. 'Here you go.'

He made no comment as he watched her pour herself a virginal glass of soda water, for which she was grateful. She supposed she could have come up with some snappy answer at a pinch, but the fewer demands made on her reserves of serenity, the better.

They took their drinks back to the verandah, Lauren leading the way, barefoot and holding on to her *kain* for dear life. As she was quite naked underneath it it would be awkward should it slip off. Of course if she were one of those daring, forward females, she would *make* it happen. Seemingly accidentally she would stub her toe or trip over a little rock or crack and let out a delicate cry of pain. Joel would grab her arm to steady her, and as she reached out to him to keep her balance, the material would slip from its knot, *et voilà*, she was naked in his arms. After that it was easy. Of course he wouldn't be able to contain himself with her disrobed against his chest. His coolness would crack like splintering ice, which would then melt and go up in steam in the heat of his passion.

She clutched the *kain* tightly to her body.

At this stage in the game she wasn't good in the role of seducer. She'd much prefer to be the seducee. Not that there was much chance of that; she might as well wish for the moon.

The *kain* securely tight around her, she sat down

again and tucked her feet underneath her. Joel began to talk about the visit he had made to the laboratories in Japara and she concentrated on what he was saying with the strength of despair. Joel was out of reach. He showed no romantic inclinations towards her; they might as well talk about the creatures of the deep sea. Her soda water tasted like nothing. She should have mixed it with a little Campari. After all, what harm could a little watered-down Campari do her? It never had yet, so why should it now?

Until a few minutes ago she had done quite well. She had had herself reasonably under control. Now she could feel the feelings flow back into her.

Her eyes were glued to Joel's face, intent on seeing every change in his expression, every little smile, every spark in his eyes. Slowly she was thawing out inside. There was something about the tone of his voice, the sound of his laughter, the way he moved his hand when he talked. He seemed so relaxed, so comfortable in her chair on her verandah . . . how could he possibly want to leave? She wanted him to get up, take her hand and lead her into the bedroom. She wanted him to kiss her and untie the *kain*, and she wanted him to make love to her.

His eyes met hers and her heart began to pound. Her nerves jangled. There was something in his eyes, a knowing, an answering of feeling. She realised she was holding her breath. The silence was electric with tension. A deep sadness filled her. Her eyes were dry, but it seemed that in that terrible silence her heart was overflowing with tears. Joel did not belong to her; why then did she feel that he was hers? That he was deserting her?

A melancholy melody floated through her mind—the music she had played so many times. Helpless sorrow suffused her. She wanted to reach out to him, but her hands did not move as if she knew she would only grasp empty air.

Joel stood up slowly, as if moving in a dream. He smiled at her, but it was only his usual, normal little smile.

'Time for me to scurry back into my dark corner,' he said lightly. 'Thank you for the drink.' Then he was gone.

For a long time Lauren sat in the chair without moving. He had known her thoughts. Not even her mind was a private place.

Lauren's next trip took her away for a week. Her driver, Amir, was with her, as was her assistant, Tiur, and the three of them travelled in the Toyota through the dry countryside. The narrow roads were clogged with traffic of buses and ox-carts and horse-carts and motorcycles and smoke-belching old trucks loaded down with mattresses or bamboo or sacks of rice. They went from village to village, meeting groups of women and visiting local government officials to make arrangements for the coming training programme. There was a lot of work to do, a lot of thinking and talking and planning, most of it in Indonesian, which kept her mind operating at top capacity.

There were the inevitable little offices, stuffy, hot and crowded. The inevitable *teh botol*, bottled tea sweet as sugar syrup and lukewarm. The inevitable little cardboard boxes filled with snacks—rice and meat mixtures wrapped in banana leaves; sticky, glutinous little cakes; sweet concoctions that looked like lumps of pink and white spaghetti. At night they ate dinner of fried rice and skewered meat or fried chicken in a village *warung* lit by kerosene lamps.

Every night she fell into bed (some lumpy bed in some small hotel in some small town) and dropped into sleep like a rock sinking to the bottom of a pond.

Concentrating on other people's problems is a good way to forget your own, or at least push them into the background. But as soon as Lauren arrived home, they came zeroing in on her with the accuracy of a rocket.

She craved some English conversation, some entertainment, some company, but she was afraid that wherever she might show her face, Joel would appear, and she couldn't bear the thought of spending the evening in his proximity.

So she didn't go to the swimming pool on Sunday. She didn't attend the Hash on Monday. She didn't even go jogging any more. Like a hermit, she spent her time locked in her bedroom, studying Indonesian, working, or reading, and feeling a growing sense of isolation.

It was of course an untenable situation. Before the week was out she'd be stark raving mad. But before the week was out Joel would be on a plane, and she hoped she could survive until then.

The day he left Lauren sat on the bed surrounded by books, magazines, paper, felt-tip pens, cracker crumbs and empty water glasses, and broke into tears. It was a luxury she had not permitted herself since the choking incident, and she let herself go with total abandon.

How could she possibly live next door to him and his wife and two little children? They would be everywhere. There would be welcome coffees and welcome teas and welcome dinners and welcome parties, and she'd be invited to many of them. She would have to be nice to the woman and smile at her and make pleasant conversation and tell her that she could call on her any time she needed something. After all, Sharon was her neighbour, and it would be convenient to pop in and ask for the name of a doctor or where to find pork chops in the Chinese market. But Lauren was at the office till mid-afternoon, so maybe it wouldn't be so bad.

But bad enough, no matter what. She'd still be seeing her many places, there was no avoiding that. Seeing Joel would be even worse.

The more she thought about Sharon, the more she didn't like her. Sharon had latched on to Joel as if he were a lifesaver. Lauren could see it in her mind: poor pathetic creature, helpless and destitute, with large doe eyes and trembling lips. (She conveniently forgot that Joel had called her 'full of spark'.) And Joel, like a true gentleman, had rushed to her side, and was marrying her now to protect her from the big bad world.

Lauren cried some more.

She didn't like herself any more, either. She was nasty and uncharitable and unfair and jealous and petty, and how could she have sunk so low?

And besides, who was Joel anyway? He was arrogant and opinionated and altogether too sure of himself. Who said he was anything special? She had never gone through so much agony over a man who showed so little interest in her. Why should she start now? He wasn't worth it. She didn't need him.

She couldn't stop crying.

She shed tears for another hour until no more tears would come. She was probably dehydrated. She drank a glass of water and took a shower.

Later that evening she went to the pub and played darts. She'd never done so well, throwing her darts with miraculous precision. Her team won all three games.

Lauren's depression did not get any better. Its severity actually began to worry her, but she didn't seem to be able to do anything about it. This was not at all like her; she'd never been like this before. Nothing held any interest for her any more. She didn't feel up to anything. Jogging in the morning took more energy than she had to spare, and every morning she dragged herself to the office with the greatest of efforts. She would catch herself staring unseeing and empty-headed at the Garfield poster. She would forget what she had been doing two minutes earlier. In mid-sentence she would stop talking because she couldn't remember what she had intended to say. Never had anything like this happened to her before. It was frightening.

All she wanted to do was stay in bed and not move, not talk, not do anything. The future was a big, black, gaping hole. If she didn't watch out she'd become a candidate for shock therapy.

How had this happened to her? Only a short time ago she hadn't even known Joel. The future had not really bothered her. Her life was interesting and she was happy enough. How could she have become so utterly depressed?

The answer did not occur to her until two weeks later.

Her sense of waiting, of expectation had gone. All her life she had known something special would happen to her.

Joel. She had known him longer than just a few weeks. There was no explanation for her feelings, but she knew that Joel and she were linked together in some special way. They belonged to each other. Yet he had left her.

Again the music played through her head, the same melody over and over and over. She covered her head with the pillow, but she could not make it stop. She cried all night.

A mysterious tropical virus was on a victorious tour through the town. Ed caught it, Sten had it, Josie got it. Twenty-four hours of concentrated misery—headache, nausea, fever—and presto, it was done and over with.

Lauren felt it coming. Sitting at her desk, drawing stick figures on a chart with coloured pens, illustrating the process of borrowing money from a bank and repaying it, she became aware of her queasy stomach. She had woken up with a headache and it was getting worse by the minute. She felt hot. Ed took one look at her and grinned.

'It looks like it's your turn, kid.'

'I think I'll go home,' she said weakly, rising to her feet with difficulty. She saw stars left, right and centre. Grasping the back of a chair, she tried to steady herself. Amir took her home, and she made it to the bathroom just in time.

So, she thought, as she lay in bed, my body has given up on me too. She sipped a glass of Coca-Cola. Cola was supposed to be good for nausea. Her fever got worse, and by the time it was night she was practically delirious. She had taken aspirin, but her stomach had refused to make it welcome. She was seeing things—butterflies all over the room, big, fluid globs of swirling colour everywhere. Her bed was floating through space. She was so hot, she was melting into the sheets.

Joel's face floated through her mind.

'You came back,' she said, feeling her face glowing like a light bulb. 'You came back because I'm sick.'

'Yes.'

'You didn't marry her, after all, did you?'

'No, I didn't marry her, after all.'

She tried to touch him, but she couldn't. Her arms waved through space like car antennae swaying in the wind.

'We belong together,' she said. 'We're connected, you and I.'

'Soulmates.'

'Yes, yes—soulmates.'

They were bound together by a kinship of the spirit, for ever and ever till the end of time. In the depths of her being she had always known him, always loved him. Timeless love.

It was a beautiful thought. A sense of peace stole over her and she fell asleep, smiling.

When she woke up she still had a fever. Yanti brought her hot tea and changed the soaked sheets. Then she had run the bath with cool water and Lauren shakily climbed into it and rested her head on the edge. She didn't stay in long. With another cup of tea and some dry crackers she settled between the cool, clean sheets. She sipped carefully and munched tiny bits of cracker, trying to keep her stomach under control. This time it co-operated—a good sign. Lauren fell asleep again. Three hours later she woke up and the fever had all but gone and she felt reborn.

Something very strange had happened. She thought of Joel and felt no despair. Everything would turn out all right. She knew, somehow, that he would not marry Sharon.

The next time she saw him, he was at the pub, playing darts and looking as if someone had put a death curse on him.

CHAPTER FIVE

HE was leaning against the wall waiting for his turn. He looked up as Lauren came in and she felt the familiar shock go through her. His eyes held hers as she walked up to him. He looked terrible.

'Hello, Joel. You're back.'

'Hello, Lauren.' His voice sounded oddly toneless.

She glanced around. No five-foor-four blonde. The only blonde was Sten's wife, short, sweet and sporty in knee-length pants and a cotton-knit top. Joel moved away from the wall and took his turn. The darts hit right where he wanted them. Whatever it was that bothered him did not affect his aim. He finished the game.

He strode right out of the door, without a word to anyone, drawing a few curious glances. Lauren followed him out. He was jamming the keys into the door of his Toyota and looked up when he noticed her standing near him.

'Don't *you* start in on me too, for God's sake!'

His uncharacteristic explosiveness shocked her into momentary silence. She was actually gaping at him. Then she felt her hackles rise.

'Don't you shout at me! I haven't said a thing, have I?'

With a vicious jerk he opened the door. 'Why did you follow me out here?'

'I didn't analyse it! I just did!' Her legs were shaking and she felt angry and scared and confused.

He got into the driver's seat and stuck the key in the ignition. 'Well, *I* know why! And let me satisfy your curiosity: Sharon is not here. The wedding was cancelled and the relationship terminated.' The engine roared into life like an angry lion. Lauren stepped aside and the car screeched out of the parking lot.

She should have been overjoyed, giddy with relief, filled with elation. But she felt none of these things. All she could think of was the anger in his voice and the tiredness of his features. Apparently this state of affairs had done nothing for his good humour. It was not a development he considered positive. There were a thousand questions milling around in her head, but she had a feeling that the answers were not forthcoming.

Slowly she went back inside and ordered a Campari and soda at the bar. Anne Furgeson was sitting at the other side and Lauren could hear her excited voice gushing out the gossip. She had it all figured out—an entire theory about the Joel issue, full of nasty innuendoes. Lauren felt like pouring her drink over her perfectly coifed head. She was a parasite, a vulture in colourful plumage.

Lauren left, to save herself.

She didn't see Joel again for days. She went to work, did battle with Ed, ate, slept, and dreamed of Joel. How long could she go on, knowing him to be in the house next to hers, alone? Not knowing what he was doing and how he was feeling made her restless and irritable. A day came when she could no longer wait, no longer just sit and think.

The path to his house seemed endless. Her heart hammered wildly and her hands were clenched with tension. As she rounded the house, she saw him sitting on the verandah wearing denim shorts and a Hash House Harrier's T-shirt. He looked up and watched her as she approached him. When she reached the three steps leading up to the verandah she stopped.

'Hi,' she said, feeling like an intruder.

'Hi,' He put his magazine down on his lap. *The Far Eastern Review*, she noticed. Her eyes caught a big black square of printer's ink where censors had been at work. 'Come on up,' he invited.

She skipped up the steps. 'Haven't seen you for a while,' she said lightly. 'Thought I'd see how you are.'

'I'm fine, thanks.'

He looked fine. His old normal cool calm self.

She was twittering with nerves. 'I'm sorry about . . . I mean . . .' she began clumsily, 'I'm sorry your trip to the States didn't work out the way you wanted.' She felt like a little girl trying to apologise to the school principal for some incomprehensible sin.

Joel's eyebrows went up. 'Are you?' he asked quietly.

She could feel the colour drain from her face. Her heart turned over. She stared at him, saying nothing.

'Sit down, Lauren.'

'No, I have to go.' She turned, nearly tripping as she stumbled down the steps and hurried down the driveway. She felt humiliated, as if some dirty little secret had been revealed. She felt exposed. He had known about her feelings for him for quite a while, she was sure, but he had not acknowledged it in words. Now it was open between them, and she had never felt quite so vulnerable.

'Lauren!'

He was behind her, grasped her shoulders and stopped her.

'Let go of me!' she said fiercely.

He turned her around to face him, leaving his hands right where they were. 'I didn't mean to upset you,' he said.

'Apology accepted,' she said with as much composure as she could muster. 'Now let me go.'

There was an instant change in him, a flaring up of light in the grey eyes. He didn't release her. Instead he pulled her to him, sliding his arms around her shoulders and bending his face to hers. His mouth found hers and he kissed her with a hard, angry passion that made her body tremble in response. He pressed her tightly against him and she could feel in him the strength and the desire and the anger.

She hated him for his violence. She loved him and she wanted him, and she had never known this mixture of conflicting emotions. She wanted to cry out and hit him. He was hurting her with his brute force. He was hurting her with his anger.

When he finally released her she was out of breath and shivering. He took a step back and they gazed at each other in silence.

She felt a strange sadness set in, a sense of utter helplessness. 'I don't know why you're so angry,' she said unsteadily. 'I don't understand why I make you so angry. It's always there, isn't it? Even when it doesn't show, I know it's there. I can feel it.'

Dusk was falling fast. They were standing in the fading light with all the colours changing into greys and blacks and deep purples. Soon pale stars would be visible in the darkening sky.

'I'm sorry,' Joel said tonelessly, 'I shouldn't have done that. I don't know what got into me.' He came closer, and to her surprise, put his arms around her again, leaning his head against hers as if weary and tired.

'I'm sorry,' he said again.

'It's all right.' There was a gentleness in his embrace and she felt a surge of tenderness. 'Why are you so angry with me?' she asked softly.

'I don't know. I think, sometimes, I'm really angry with myself.'

'But because of me?'

'Yes.'

'But why?'

'I wish I knew. I don't know, I don't understand it.'

Lauren didn't understand it either. What had she done? What had she said? She couldn't think clearly at all with Joel so close. The smell and the feel and the

warmth of his body filled her with a helpless yearning.
She moved her face and her cheek rubbed against his
chin. He lowered his mouth, his lips brushing the corner
of her mouth.

'Lauren,' he whispered, 'let me do this again.'

The touch of his lips covering hers shivered through
her. His kiss, this time, was gentle and tender and she
felt weak with longing. Her pulses raced. She belonged
to him. He was hers.

A certainty beyond doubt.

She loved him and she wanted him and she would do
anything to make him love her, but she had no idea
what she needed to do. All she could do now was to
stand there in his arms with her mouth clinging to his,
hoping he would never stop, never go away from her,
hoping he would fill up the loneliness inside her. Give
her back some peace.

He kissed her at length, his mouth warm and
persuasive, and she responded without restraint,
releasing all her pent-up emotions of love and desire
and need. She could feel his heart beat against her
breast. Nothing but clamouring senses, sweet longing,
and the darkness settling softly around them.

Was this again a dream? An illusion with roots in her
secret longings? Were the stars up high again the stars
of another night? Was this a glimpse of memory her
mind refused to reveal?

But when Joel released her and smiled into her eyes,
she knew it had not been. He was here with her and he
had held her and kissed her and it had all been real. His
one arm was still around her shoulders and he began to
lead her back towards the house.

They walked in silence. There was a harmony
between them, and the spell that enveloped them made
her feel drunk with happiness.

They went into the house. 'Let's have something to
eat,' he suggested.

Lauren thought of the meal Yanti was preparing. She'd better give her a call.

'I'd like that.' Tonight she would eat here and talk to him and listen to his voice and his laughter, watch him smile.

They were alone in the house. His cook had gone to the *kampong* to attend the wedding of a friend. The kitchen was small and inadequate, like her own, and they stood close together as they prepared a feast of shrimp-filled avocadoes, different kinds of cheese, crusty French bread, sliced mangoes and starfruit.

They sat on the verandah. Joel had spread a white cloth over the table and lit a small, old-fashioned oil lamp. There was wine to go with the meal and they clinked their glasses and toasted to each other's health and happiness.

Lauren had sat like this with other men, at a festive table full of good food and wine and burning candles, but it had never been like this. She had never felt this deep, intense happiness. From the house Vivaldi's music drifted towards them. Perfection.

They talked about music and books, about life and the dreams of their childhood, their hopes and wishes. They talked about the flowers he had given her at the party.

'I did mind, you know,' she said, smiling a little now at the memory. 'It seems so silly, but I didn't like the idea of you giving me funeral flowers, even though I had bought the same ones myself that very morning.'

'I was sorry, too, later. But it never crossed my mind until it was too late. They were beautiful, and that's all I thought about at the time.'

Their hands touched on the table.

'You're a strange woman,' he said, stroking her fingers. 'I keep thinking this isn't real—that you're not really you and that I'm not really me, that somehow we're only playing a part.'

'Why?' Her voice sounded strange. They weren't playing a part. She didn't want to believe that.

'I feel . . . at peace.'

Lauren didn't understand. 'Being yourself you wouldn't be at peace?'

It seemed as if, for a moment, he hesitated. 'I haven't been at peace for a very long time, only I never admitted it to myself.' He was holding her hand between both of his now and she felt suffused with love. She wanted this to be real, this feeling between them, not some illusion that would dissolve as soon as they parted. She wanted this to last.

'But this is real,' she said, 'that's why you feel at peace.' There was a quietness, a serenity in her too, and in a way it seemed odd that it should be that way sitting here with Joel who had caused her so much confusion and despair in the past two months.

'It's more like a dream,' he said quietly. 'And when I wake up, it's all gone.'

'No.' She shook her head. 'No.' She stood up and moved to the other side of the table where he sat. She knelt in front of him and put her head on his knees. 'I'm real. Hold me. Touch me.'

He put his hands on her head and stroked her hair. 'Don't you see?' he said softly. 'The real Lauren, the Lauren I know, would never do this.'

'Maybe you don't know me very well.'

He didn't reply, but went on stroking her hair, gently, rhythmically, until finally he came to his feet, pulling her with him. He drew her against him and she put her arms around him and kissed him. Fire leaped between them, the intensity almost frightening. She drew back, not knowing why.

The Vivaldi concerto came to an end and they looked at each other in the sudden silence. It was a strange, breathless moment.

They had coffee laced with Kahlua and for a while they sat in silent harmony listening to the night sounds around them, the whispering of the palms, the rustling of some nocturnal creature, the funny cry of a lizard.

'How long have we known each other?' Joel asked suddenly. He wasn't looking at her, his gaze directed at the stars.

'For a long time.' It had only been a couple of months.

'Yes, it seems that way.'

'The first time I met you, I felt that way.'

He scanned her face. 'You said we'd met before.'

'I thought so. You were so familiar to me, I don't know why, but you did.'

'You thought we'd met in Spain.'

She nodded, looking down on her hands. 'Yes.' Her voice was a husky whisper.

'You know, Lauren, it was true when I said I'd never been to Spain.'

'I know. I. . . .' Tears came to her eyes. The old familiar sadness washed over her again. She couldn't go on and she fell silent.

'Are you crying?' There was surprise in his voice. She heard him get up and a moment later he was drawing her up into his arms. 'Tell me about it,' he said gently.

'I've never been to Spain either,' she whispered miserably. 'Can you believe it? It frightens me, because I'm so sure. I *know* there's a connection between you and me, and I *know* Spain has something to do with it. It isn't normal . . . I mean, it's crazy. Where do I get these notions? It can't be!'

'Maybe we've met in another life.'

She stood still in his arms, incredulous. 'Do you believe in that sort of thing?'

'No.' There was a smile in his voice. 'But some people do, and who's to say who's right? We could pretend, couldn't we?'

She shook her head. 'No. My feelings are real. There has to be some reason for them.'

'There probably is, only you don't know it yet. It'll come to you one day—some simple explanation. A movie you've seen, a book you've read. Maybe a dream.'

She'd thought about the same things herself, but she still wasn't convinced.

'Not everything in life has a simple explanation.' She gave a watery smile. 'Sounds like the truth of the century, doesn't it?'

Joel kissed her lightly. 'Maybe it doesn't matter. It's the feelings that count, not the explanations. Don't worry about it.'

Maybe she was reading too much into this evening, into the words spoken and the glances and the smiles. Tomorrow in the daylight this evening might have lost its significance. Maybe it meant nothing that she was in his arms wanting so very much to be loved by him, to have him hold her and kiss her and speak tender words.

Feelings. What was real? What wasn't? Not long ago he had boarded a plane to marry another woman. Now he was here with her and she was no longer sure about him, about herself. She was tired and confused and she could no longer think clearly.

She wanted to go home.

When she told him, he took her hand and walked her back to the empty house with the big bed in the bare room.

She lay in bed, knowing she had never felt more lonely.

It had been a wonderful evening in many ways, but her feelings were mixed and chaotic. On Friday she went to play darts, thinking the pub would be a good place to see Joel again. They would be surrounded by people and laughter and the sounds of darts hitting the board, glasses tinkling, and the radio emitting soft music. Neutral territory.

What's the matter with me? she wondered.

Joel was sitting at the bar. Anne Furgeson was occupying the stool next to him, her black hair shining silkily in the dim light. She was talking to Joel, giving him a devastating smile just as Lauren approached them.

Joel turned. 'Hello, Lauren. Sit down.' He patted the empty stool on his other side. 'What can I get you?'

She sat down, said she'd like a Campari and soda, and caught the hostile look in Anne's eyes. The lady wanted Joel to herself.

'Where's your husband?' Lauren asked politely.

Anne shrugged smoothly tanned shoulders and waved a careless hand towards the players. 'Over there, doing his thing.'

'Oh, I hadn't noticed him.'

'That's easy to do.'

Lauren did not comment, but she felt a surge of intense loathing. She glanced at Joel, who pretended not to have heard. Cool, calm, and unperturbed. Anne was the most miserable female she'd ever encountered—vicious, nasty, bitchy.

Lauren reached for the peanuts and Joel's hand came out and covered hers for a moment.

'Careful,' he said softly, so only she could hear.

She nodded. Anne was watching them, her eyes full of pure venom. Smiling at her innocently, Lauren slid off her stool, taking her drink with her. She stood with the players and watched the game in progress. Anne did not threaten her one bit.

Moments later, Joel joined her. 'My God,' he whispered, 'that woman is a pain in the neck! What's the matter with her?'

'She hates her husband and she wants your body.'

He groaned. 'I was afraid of that. Just what I need, a married woman with a heart constructed of barbed wire!'

'She's beautiful,' she said, to see how he would react.

He gave her a look of such exasperation that she burst out laughing.

'Thank God you're not serious,' he said.

'She *is* beautiful.'

'So is my dentist. Who the hell cares when she has a tongue spitting acid?'

'What has she been telling you?'

'Everything. She was playing the analyst, lots of fancy psychological jargon, tearing apart everybody in this room, including her husband, who is, according to her, a lousy lover.'

'You should have told her a man needs a good woman to be a good lover.'

He laughed so hard that everybody looked at them.

'Did she say anything about me?' Lauren asked. 'I'd be fascinated to know.'

Joel grinned. 'No, she didn't dare.'

'She'll be saying her piece to others, no doubt.' Especially after the poisonous looks she had bestowed on her this evening.

Joel shrugged. 'I suppose people know her.'

'Surprisingly, a number of people think she's charming.' It was true. Why, Lauren had no idea. Maybe Anne had multiple personalities.

They played a game of darts, talking and laughing between turns. Joel gave her some pointers about her throw, holding her wrist to show her. She liked the firmness of his fingers. Even the simplest touch set off a reaction in her. Right then and there she wanted to put her arms around him and hold him. When he smiled into her eyes, she was afraid people would see her glow.

They played two games and when the last one was finished they left together. They had come in separate cars and he walked with her to hers. He waited until she had climbed in and started the engine, then wished her goodnight, kissing her on the cheek through the open window.

Lauren drove off, disappointment bitter inside her. Why hadn't he asked her to come with him? She didn't want to go home alone. She wanted to be with him. The intimate dinner on the verandah of his house had meant nothing—a pleasant interlude at the most. It was obvious he had no intention of diving head first into a love affair with her.

Lauren sighed. It was ridiculous to hope that he would want to. He had just come out of a close relationship with another woman, broken up on the steps of the church, practically. He was biding his time. She should appreciate the fact that his emotions weren't so shallow as to flutter from one woman to another in a matter of weeks.

She parked the car in the garage and closed the doors. What had transpired between Joel and Sharon? It seemed utterly romantic to think that he had broken up with her because he had fallen in love with her, Lauren, but for some reason she didn't believe that to be the case. There was something else involved, but she didn't know what.

The house was dark and lonely. She switched the light on in the bedroom and thoughtfully began to peel off her clothes. Maybe Sharon had found herself another man while Joel was traipsing around the East. That sort of thing happened often enough.

But she knew that that wasn't it, either.

Life became very hectic. Joel was in Jakarta for several days and before he returned Lauren had to leave for a week-long training programme in Solo. She was involved in the arrangements and her mind was going five different directions. Fifty people from all over the area had to be accommodated for a week. A conference room had been found and rented. It needed to be set up so they could give their presentations with the help of the charts and visual aids Lauren had prepared. They

needed stands and a place on the wall to hang up maps
and charts. The details were legion and she hated
running around doing trivial things that somehow no
one else had considered, thought of, or taken care of.

The conference room had been decorated with potted
plants and large flower arrangements in bright colours.
Windows opened up on both sides, and Lauren hoped
there would be a breeze so they wouldn't all suffocate.
Every day refreshments would be served in small
cardboard boxes—some sort of sticky cake and varying
kinds of meat and rice mixtures wrapped in banana
leaves, and of course the syrupy *teh botol* was ever-
present. Lunch too was served in boxes, a layer of rice
topped with a tasty mixture of meat and vegetables,
usually spicy.

At times like this she always remembered the
convention centre she had once visited in California
where big corporations held their annual bashes—an
entire complex of conference rooms, motel rooms,
restaurants, and well-equipped exercise rooms complete
with sauna, jacuzzi and pool. There were tennis courts,
a golf course and an olympic-size outdoor pool with
loungers and tables and a well-stocked bar. The centre
boasted a beauty parlour where glamorous girls would
do your hair and your face and your nails. They would
wax your legs and give you a body massage and do
whatever you wanted done to beautify or purify the
body.

The motel rooms featured big, comfortable beds with
built-in massage devices that required no coins. They had
colour TV, beautiful, sterile bathrooms with soaps and
shampoos and bath oils of the most luxurious brands. The
rooms contained a small refrigerator stocked with drinks
and ice and snacks. Coffee and tea were supplied as well as
the little machine to brew them in.

The air-conditioned conference rooms came complete
with chalkboards, screens, projectors, microphones,

recording machines, paper, pencils, and comfortable, upholstered chairs.

Lauren remembered wandering through the gorgeous, meticulously manicured gardens that surrounded the place, thinking that all that opulence might be nice and convenient, but how boring it would be to spend too much time there. It was all too perfect and plastic and artificial.

But secretly, as she was running around in frustration organising her programme, she couldn't help wishing for some of the amenities of that California pleasure palace. Still, she loved the challenge of what she was doing. It stimulated and excited her and made her a nervous wreck. And when it was all done, she knew the thrill of success, the sense of satisfaction after a job well done. She'd never trade that feeling for anything.

Lauren's hotel happened to be close to a small mosque, and she was awakened by the muezzin wailing out over the neighbourhood at the godforsaken hour of three in the morning and again at five. Her sleep was fitful, her mind restless, her bed uncomfortable, the room hot, her nerves frayed.

Today was the first day of the programme, and as always she felt a terrible case of stage fright. She had done this sort of thing countless times, in different countries and in different places on Java, and still every time insecurity plagued her. So many things could go wrong. Each country, province, district had its own customs and procedures and formalities. What worked in one place was a disastrous fiasco in another.

In the pale dawn of morning on that first day she knew that this time everything would go wrong. She would be a failure in front of fifty Javanese. They would not understand her pathetic Indonesian, would make no sense of her charts and drawings. She thought this every time. She glanced around the bare little room and wondered why she had got herself in this situation, in this profession.

She should be back home, married to some nice man from Iowa and taking care of a house and two children and be a teacher's aide at the local school or decorate cakes at the bakery. She would never have to wonder whether her Indonesian was adequate, or worry about her performance at a training programme. She would never have to drink *teh botol* again. She was conveniently forgetting the worries of that other life—mortgage payments and doctors' bills and broken-down washing machines and overworked husbands who yelled at the kids.

She got up and dressed.

The morning was full of ceremony. Dignitaries came and welcomed the participants and showered praise. The Javanese love formality. There were long speeches, prayers, and more speeches. There was an endless hand-shaking procession—everybody lining up and shaking hands with everybody. Lauren felt conspicuous and out of place, sticking out head and shoulders above everyone else.

As the day progressed, her sense of doom evaporated. She concentrated on what she was doing and forgot everything else.

The week passed without major disasters. All went actually amazingly well.

After she returned home, she slept for twelve hours straight, purging body and soul of strain and stress. She felt reborn, got out of bed and went out to get a cup of tea. Then she did some stretching exercises and went for a three-mile jog. She was almost back home when she noticed another runner coming down the road. Joel. Her heart leaped. She stopped and waited.

He grinned and grunted a good-morning, breathing hard and perspiring profusely. Lauren was soaked to the skin herself and her hair hung in wet peaks along her cheeks. She tugged them behind her ears. Yuk, she needed a shower!

'So you're back,' he said with difficulty, his chest rising and falling rapidly. 'How did it go?'

'Fine. I'll tell you all about it if you'll have breakfast with me.' It was Sunday; they had all the time in the world.

'I look that appealing?'

'About as appealing as I do. I'll let you go home to have a shower first.'

'It's a deal.' His smile was devastating. He looked wonderful and healthy and sporty, and she didn't mind the sweat.

'See you in a little while, then.' She smiled back brightly, feeling light and glowing. Sunday morning and he'd have breakfast with her! Life wasn't so bad.

She showered and shampooed and blow-dried her hair, standing naked in front of the mirror. What would he think of her body? Oh, the age-old worries! Would he think her legs too long? Her hips not rounded enough? Her breasts too small? Was there ever a woman content with her shape?

Her hair was long and thick and it took quite a while to dry, and in that time she had analysed and criticised and scrutinised every inch of her body. Nothing was right. Joel couldn't possibly find her sexy, desirable, lovable. Never mind that other men had found her so. *He* wouldn't—*didn't*.

She sighed a sad sigh and put the hair dryer away, thinking that if ever, *ever* they'd make love, they'd have to do it in the dark. And she wouldn't take her nightgown off and she'd tell him to shut his eyes and not look at her.

She laughed out loud at herself, at the idea of acting like a Victorian virgin on her wedding night. Putting on white shorts and a sea-green silk shirt, she glanced in the mirror again and decided she looked quite presentable with her skin glowing with health, her eyes laughing, her hair shining. She wasn't so bad after all. She could even cook!

That morning she was at her best. Yanti was off on Sundays and Lauren cooked breakfast herself. A slice of sweet papaya sprinkled with lime juice, a fluffy omelette filled with cheese and tomatoes and mushrooms. The toast was perfect, the coffee aromatic. The cassette player emitted sensuous waves of sound.

'Ah, the lady can cook,' said Joel, as he tasted the first bite of omelette.

'I can type too,' she said, looking smug.

'Perfection all the way around, I can tell.' His eyes sparked humour.

She thought of herself in front of the mirror an hour ago, full of self-criticism and self-doubt.

'You wouldn't believe what happened to me this morning,' said Joel after he'd finished his toast. 'A goose chased me as I ran around the park. He was really going for me, neck stuck out and racing at top speed!'

The image of Joel being chased by a goose made her laugh. They took their second cup of coffee out on the verandah where it was still reasonably cool because of the breeze. They sat there for an hour and Lauren told him about her week. He listened with interest, asking questions. She told him about Ed, too, about his condescending behaviour that gave her fits. He didn't laugh or try to treat it with humour or find excuses for Ed's words and actions. She liked it.

The same sort of thing was happening to Sharon, too, he said. He recounted some of her experiences in the school system which involved the school principal and some of the board members. Sharon, who was a calm and quiet person, had in her own unperturbed way fought back and given the men something to think about without ever making them angry. He told her the story in an even tone, and Lauren couldn't help but admire the woman's insight and tactics. Her mental picture of Sharon as a clinging vine or weeping willow was proving to be rather inaccurate, to say the least.

Joel loved her, or had loved her. He wasn't the kind of man who would go for the clinging vine variety, she should have known that. For a while they were both absorbed in their own thoughts, and she gazed absently at the dry grass of the lawn and thought about Sharon.

'Did it hurt very much?' she asked at last. 'Breaking up with her?'

He didn't immediately reply and she was angry at herself for having asked the question. She had no right to ask anything so personal.

'Yes,' he said finally, his voice even, 'for a while it hurt like hell, but I got over it.'

It didn't make sense. If something was bad it would not go away in a matter of weeks. Broken hearts didn't heal that fast.

He gave her a lopsided smile. 'You see, it was a mutual mistake. Marriage was not for us. I didn't see it, not consciously, but Sharon had the insight and the courage to stop before it was too late. We sat up an entire night and just talked.'

'You were apart for six months or so. You were in Surabaya before you came here, weren't you?'

He nodded. 'The separation helped to make things clear to her, she said.'

Lauren's mouth felt dry. 'You told me you loved her,' she said without looking at him. She was afraid to see something she didn't want to see.

There was a short silence. 'I did—I still do. There are many kinds of love.' He paused, looking out over the garden. 'She'll always be my friend.'

Lauren glanced at his hands holding the empty coffee cup. She'd made more coffee and she leaned forward to pour them both some more. 'What kind of person is she? I think my mental picture of her is all wrong.' Over the coffee pot his eyes met hers and he smiled.

'How did you imagine her?'

'I'd rather not say.' She grinned sheepishly. 'It wasn't very flattering.'

There was unconcealed amusement in his eyes now. Did he guess her thoughts?

'Sharon is a very strong, independent person. She made her own way after her husband left her, had her babies by herself, found a small apartment, went to work when the boys were two months old and somehow kept her sanity through it all.'

'Did you know her then?'

He nodded. 'I watched her go through it all, without any help—she didn't want any. But I took her out sometimes to get her away for a few hours, and after work I would drop in and have coffee and talk, or more often watch her as she took care of the babies and cooked dinner. Sometimes I'd just keep her company at night while she was correcting papers.'

There was a constricted feeling in Lauren's chest. 'Sounds like a cosy set-up to me. Would it have been so bad to be married to her if you got along so well?'

He raked his hand through his hair. 'All the reasons were wrong—I know that now. Our relationship suited our needs of the moment. We were both lonely and in need of some companionship. I'd been running around the world for years and it was the first time I was home for any length of time. I'd begun to feel too restless and unsettled and I'd taken a teaching job at the university. I wanted to see if I'd like a more orderly life. I wanted a sense of permanency, and Sharon could give me that, I thought. In the long run our relationship wouldn't have worked out, I know that now. But for that time in our lives it was good the way it was. We needed each other.' He paused, lost in thought for a moment. 'She said to me, "I know you like me and respect me and trust me,

Joel, but I don't think you ever really loved me." I said she was wrong. I did love her, but I suppose it was not the right kind of love. I'd really wanted to marry her because I wanted to settle down. I wanted a family.'

'What about the boys? Did they know about your plans?'

He shook his head. 'We hadn't told them. I was their honorary Uncle Joel, and I guess that's what I will be from now on.' He didn't smile.

He had looked forward to being a father, she knew. It made her sad to think he'd had to give that up too, at least for the time being.

Joel left shortly after that and she went inside to do the dishes, and to think about what he had told her. She had made a discovery that morning.

Joel was lonely too.

Friends had invited her for dinner that night. Philip was English and Gayetrie was Indian. Lauren was looking forward to the evening because she loved curries and they'd be treated to an authentic Indian meal with all the trimmings.

Music floated towards her as she walked through the door. Someone was playing the piano, playing her favourite piece, *Memories*. For a moment she couldn't move. Then like an automaton, she crossed the room to say hello to Gayetrie, who was resplendent in a green silk sari and gold jewellery. A drink was put into her hand and she talked and smiled, while all the time all she really heard were the familiar notes floating around her. No piano in sight. Someone was playing in another room. She had to find out who, and where.

Slipping out on to the verandah, she followed the sounds. Through an open window the music flowed towards her, enveloping her. She stood still and listened, almost in a trance, feeling again the sadness and the melancholy it always aroused in her. It was part of her, this music, stirring the depths of her being, revealing a secret core of emotion.

She looked through the window. It was Joel sitting at the piano, his back towards her. No one else was in the room. It was a study with bookshelves along the walls, a large desk, a brass lamp and the piano. One door led out into the house, the other on to the verandah where she was standing in the dark.

My music! she thought. How well he played it! Did he feel any of the emotions she did? The sadness rose inside her until it caught in her throat and tears came into her eyes. The music came to an end then, the last notes trailing away forlornly, and the emptiness it left was overwhelming.

Suddenly Joel was next to her in the silent darkness. She tried to control her trembling limbs. The breeze touched her face and it felt cold and wet. Her throat was locked and not a word would come. He touched her arm.

'I knew you were here,' he said softly. 'I knew you were listening.'

'You couldn't see me.' The words struggled out of her throat and her voice sounded thick.

'I sensed it. It was very strange.' His fingers touched her face 'Why are you crying?'

'The music . . . it's beautiful. You played it very well.'

'And it made you cry?'

She nodded. 'It always does that. It's my favourite piece of music.'

There was a strange silence. She took a deep breath, trying to find a semblance of composure, wishing he would take her in his arms and hold her close. The silence stretched and her nerves grew taut with apprehension.

'Lauren,' he said at last, sounding very odd, 'that's impossible.'

'I don't know what you mean.'

His hands rested on her shoulders and he regarded her closely. 'It can't be your favourite music,' he said quietly. 'There's no way in the world that you can know that piece. You must be mistaken.'

She swallowed. 'I know every note.'

A motionless silence surrounded them. Not a leaf stirred, not a creature moved. His breathing was the only sound, the warmth of his hands on her shoulders the only sensation. His eyes looked deep into hers. She felt suspended in time.

'I wrote that music myself,' he said slowly. 'It hasn't been recorded or published. No one has ever played it but me.'

Everything seemed unreal. 'I know it,' she whispered. 'I've played it many times.'

So many times. By heart. From the heart. And always with the same bittersweet longing for something unknown, yet remembered with emotion.

It had been Joel she had been waiting for all these years, Joel she had recognised with some mysterious part of her consciousness.

'Play it for me.' Joel's hands left her shoulders.

Lauren slid past him into the room. She sat down on the stool and touched her fingers to the keys, closing her eyes.

It was there in her fingers as it had always been, pouring forth from a deep and secret place inside her. She played the music as she had done so many times, losing herself in it, feeling the melancholy sadness surrounding her, filling the room.

After she had finished she sat quietly for a while, her fingers still resting lightly on the keyboard. It had always taken her a while to transport herself back to reality. Then she turned slowly, seeing Joel leaning against the desk, his face very pale.

For a long time he did not speak, just stood there observing her with dark, unfamiliar eyes. A cold shiver ran down her spine.

'Where did you get that music, Lauren?'

She shrugged helplessly. 'I have no idea. It's such a long time ago. . . .'

'A long time ago?'

'I don't remember when I learned to play it. I was a child. It seems I've always known it. I've played it so many times. I don't even remember ever seeing it on paper. I don't remember who composed it, either.'

He straightened away from the desk and came towards her. Taking her hands, he drew her up from the stool and she moved as in a trance. Standing so close to him now, seeing every line in his face, she felt the familiar rushing of her blood, the ache inside her for his love.

'Lauren,' he said softly, very softly, '*I* wrote that music. I wrote it a few months ago, right after we met.'

She felt faint with an odd presentiment. 'It's not possible,' she whispered. 'It can't be the same music.'

'You know it is. Every last note.'

His grey eyes held hers locked and again it seemed as if all reality faded and they were in some other time and place, another sphere of consciousness. She had a curious sense of destiny, a fleeting moment of insight, then it was lost.

'How did you compose it?' she asked finally. 'Whose piano did you use?'

'I was here in this very room. I asked Philip if I could use his piano, and he gave me the key to the house because he and Gayetrie were spending a week in Singapore. No one was here to hear me. It was wonderful being alone in this room, just me and the piano. I sat down, trying out the notes that I'd carried around in my head for the last few weeks, and it was easy. It was as if it wrote itself, as if it had been in my mind for a long time and came just floating out.'

Lauren said nothing. She just stood there, motionless, letting the words settle, searching for their significance.

*It was as if it wrote itself, as if it had been in my mind for
a long time and came just floating out.*

'Maybe it was,' she said softly. 'Maybe it was in your
mind all along.'

He took her face in his hands and gazed into her
eyes. Then his mouth covered hers in a kiss that was
infinitely tender. 'Lauren,' he whispered, 'who are you?'

Who was she? Who was he? What was the connection
between them? The meaning of that beautiful, haunting
music that no one knew but the two of them?

She shook her head helplessly. 'I don't know any
more. I don't understand what's going on. Every time I
see you I wonder who *you* are.' She paused. I love you,
she wanted to say. I don't know who you are, but I've
waited for you all my life.

But she couldn't say those words. She rested her
forehead on his shoulder. 'I know you, but I can't
remember from where. I know the answer is somewhere
in my mind, but it won't come out. It's driving me
crazy!' Tears ran down her face and he tightened his
arms around her.

They stood like that for a long time, silent and in
thought.

Lauren sat through the entire dinner, eating the hot
chicken curry, the yogurt salad, the *dhal*, and tasted
nothing. Across the table from her sat Joel. His
presence was all she was aware of.

CHAPTER SIX

WHY had she expected that after that evening everything would change between them? It seemed that their relationship had entered a different, more intimate phase, but there was no change in Joel's behaviour towards her. No grand passion developed. He appeared to like her well enough, but seemed to be in no hurry to catapult into a roaring love affair.

Lauren thought of nothing else but him. Her dreams were filled with his presence. Her senses thrilled just at the thought of him.

In the beginning she wasn't aware that something was changing around her. She was too absorbed in her thoughts and dreams of Joel. Slowly she began to realise that people were looking at her in a strange way, that they didn't seem to want to talk to her when they met in the store or in the pub. She was getting the cold treatment.

Oh, come on now, Lauren, you're imagining things, she told herself.

She wasn't imagining things. Life became very quiet—no dinner invitations, no parties to go to. Something was going on, and she didn't like it. In fact it began to bother her a great deal. What had she done to be treated like a pariah all of a sudden? And she wasn't suffering from some delusion; the message was coming through loud and clear: We don't want you.

After work one day she stopped at Josie's house. She lay stretched out on the sofa, reading a book, drinking tea, and eating chocolate cake.

'Oh, it's so nice to see you!' Josie said warmly.

Well, at least somebody thought so. Lauren sat down.

Harlequin Romance

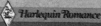
Harlequin Romance

Man of Power
Mary Wibberley

Love Beyond Reason
Karen van der Zee

GET 4 BOOKS FREE

Harlequin Romance

quin Romance

The Winds of Winter
Sandra Field

The Leo Man
Rebecca Stratton

LOVE BEYOND REASON
There was a surprise in store for Amy!

Amy had thought nothing could be as perfect as the days she had shared with Vic Hoyt in New York City—before he took off for his Peace Corps assignment in Kenya.

Impulsively, Amy decided to follow. She was shocked to find Vic established in his new life...and interested in a new girl friend.

Amy faced a choice: be smart and go home...or stay and fight for the only man she would ever love.

MAN OF POWER
Sara took her role seriously

Although Sara had already planned her esc from the subservient pos in which her father's dea had placed her, Morgan Haldane's timely appear had definitely made it e

All Morgan had asked in return was that she pose fiancée. He'd confessed needing protection from partner's wife, Louise, an part of Sara's job proved

But unfortunately for heart, Morgan ha told her about Monique...

Your Romantic Adventure Starts Here.

THE LEO MAN
"He's every bit as sexy as his father!"

Her grandmother thought that description would appeal to Rowan, but Rowan was determined to avoid any friendship with the arrogant James Fraser.

Aboard his luxury yacht, that wasn't easy. When they were all shipwrecked on a tropical island, it proved impossible.

And besides, if it weren't for James, none of them would be alive. Rowan was confused. Was it merely gratitude that she now felt for this strong and rugged man?

THE WINDS O WINTER
She'd had so much— now she had no

Anne didn't dwell on it, b the pain was still with her double-edged pain of gr and rejection.

It had greatly altered her Anne barely resembled girl who four years earlie left her husband, David. probably wouldn't even recognize her—especially with another name.

Anne made up her mind just *had* to go to his house discover if what she suspe was true...

These FOUR free Harlequin Romance novels allow you to enter the world of romance, love and desire. As a member of the Harlequin Home Subscription Plan, you can continue to experience all the moods of love. You'll be inspired by moments so real. . .so moving. . .you won't want them to end. So start your own Harlequin Romance adventure by returning the reply card below. <u>DO IT TODAY!</u>

TAKE THESE 4 BOOKS AND TOTE BAG FREE!

Mail to: Harlequin Reader Service 2504 W. Southern Avenue, Tempe, AZ 85282

YES, please send me FREE and without obligation my 4 Harlequin Romances. If you do not hear from me after I have examined my 4 FREE books, please send me the 6 new Harlequin Romances each month as soon as they come off the presses. I understand that I will be billed only $9.00 for all 6 books. There are no shipping and handling nor any other hidden charges. There is no minimum number of books that I have to purchase. In fact, I can cancel this arrangement at any time. The first 4 books and the tote bag are mine to keep as FREE gifts, even if I do not buy any additional books.

116 CIR-EAUR

NAME	(please print)	
ADDRESS		APT. NO.
CITY	STATE	ZIP

Signature (If under 18, parent or guardian must sign).

This offer is limited to one order per household and not valid to present subscribers. We reserve the right to exercise discretion in granting membership. If price changes are necessary you will be notified. Offer expires April 30, 1985.

PRINTED IN U.S.A.

EXTRA BONUS
MAIL YOUR ORDER
TODAY AND GET A
FREE TOTE BAG
FROM HARLEQUIN.

BUSINESS REPLY CARD

First Class   Permit No. 70   Tempe, AZ

POSTAGE WILL BE PAID BY ADDRESSEE

Harlequin Reader Service
2504 W. Southern Avenue,
Tempe, Arizona 85282

NO POSTAGE
NECESSARY
IF MAILED
IN THE
UNITED STATES

Josie straightened and brushed the cake crumbs from her skirt. 'Where have you been lately?'

'Home.'

Josie stared at her, then frowned. 'Would you like some tea and cake?'

'Please.'

Josie poured her a cup and cut off a big piece of cake. 'You don't look so happy,' she commented, looking distinctly uneasy.

'Because I'm not. I'd like to know what's the matter with the people in this town. Or what they think is the matter with me.' Lauren gulped her tea.

Josie smoothed her skirt over her knees, looking down on her hands and avoiding her eyes. 'I'm not sure what you mean,' she muttered nervously.

'Yes, you do! Come on, Josie! People are treating me as if I had the plague! Suddenly nobody wants to talk to me any more. Nobody invites me any more. They don't pass on the information from the Community Centre any more. There was a fund-raising dinner last week, remember? They conveniently forgot to let me know. I heard about it the next day. They don't want my money, I guess. What have I done? What's the matter with everybody?'

Josie looked agonised. 'Oh, Lauren, I feel so terrible,' she blurted out. 'I know it's not true, but they're saying all these things about you and I tried. . . .'

'Nasty things? *What* nasty things? What's going on, for heaven's sake!'

'Well, I . . . oh, it's all about you and Joel!'

About her and Joel? What could they be saying about them that was so terrible? If they were having an affair, which they were not, it would hardly qualify as a shocker. Why would anyone object? Or what else between Joel and her could cause such drastic reactions, such silent outrage?

'I haven't a clue what you mean, Josie.'

'Well, I . . . they say you broke up his marriage!'

'I broke up his marriage? He wasn't married, Josie!'

'They say it was your fault he didn't get married. That you made him change his mind.' Josie was wringing her hands. 'Oh, I know it's not true! You would never do anything like that, you're much too nice a person, but. . . .' She shrugged helplessly.

It was comforting to know she had one friend left in the town. 'I've never heard anything so ridiculous! Why does anybody even *care*? It's none of their business in the first place. And who is saying these things, anyway?'

'The girls, you know. I heard about it when we were playing bridge at Anne's house, and then soon everybody was talking about it.'

Anne, the viper! Of course, she should have guessed. Rage filled her. That woman was the most vicious, contemptible person this side of Calcutta. It was hard keeping her anger under control. Lauren dug into her cake with a vengeance, chewed, swallowed, finished her tea. Her eyes caught Josie's distraught face.

'Haven't they got anything better to do than gossip about other people? Who the hell do they think they are, anyway?' She poured herself another cup of tea.

Josie looked at her with sad eyes. Oh, poor Josie. She was suffering, Lauren could tell.

'I'm so sorry, Lauren. They . . . they don't like you very much.'

'You might call that an understatement,' she said bitterly.

'You know what I think?'

'No. What do you think?'

'I think they're jealous.'

Lauren was stunned. *'Jealous?'*

Josie nodded. 'I've thought about it a lot, you know. I heard them make all these snide remarks about how you dress and how you talk business with the men at parties to show off, and that sort of thing. Well, I just think they're jealous. You're beautiful and you have lovely clothes and you're very smart and you're free and single. You can do what you want. They just sit at home, like me, and they can't work because they can't get a permit, of course. And jobs aren't easy to find anyway, and secretly they all wish they were you.'

Dumbfounded, Lauren gaped at Josie for a full minute. 'Oh, Josie, that's terrible!' Then she began to laugh. She couldn't help it. It was so ironic, it was funny. 'You know, Josie, a lot of the time I sit at home alone, envying them because they have a husband and children and a home life. I have none of these things. It gets very lonely at times—no one to talk to, no one to eat with, no one to curl up with at night.'

Josie hesitated. 'Isn't it better now that you have Joel? I mean, you and he. . . .'

'It's not what you think, Josie. We eat together sometimes. We talk sometimes. We do not curl up together at night.'

Josie flushed with embarrassment. 'Oh, gosh! Everybody thinks you're having a torrid love affair, you two.'

'Well, now you know.'

Josie nodded thoughtfully. 'I think that made them jealous too—the fact that you caught the most handsome man in town.'

Lauren rolled her eyes in exasperation. 'They all have husbands. Do they want him too?'

'Of course,' Josie retorted, bubbling into laughter. 'I guess they get bored with their husbands.'

'You don't.'

'Mine is special.'

Lauren thought of freckled, sandy-haired Steve. She grinned. 'Oh, Josie, so are you, so are you.'

Lauren went home, raging inwardly. What she would love to do was go to Anne Furgeson's house and have a chat with her, tell her exactly what she thought of her. Of course she'd do no such thing. It wouldn't do any good anyway. Besides, she was above this petty, infantile, contemptible behaviour of Anne and her friends. They were beneath her, *beneath* her, way down there in the pit of all pits.

Brave thoughts. But the fact remained that she still was an outcast in the town. The reality of her life was that she was being criticised with self-righteous indignation. How long could she stand being treated that way? She had half a year to go before her job was finished. Could she live like a recluse, shunned by all, for that length of time? She was getting angrier and angrier and not a little bit melodramatic. Not really every soul in town was avoiding her. The men seemed as friendly as before and even a few women did acknowledge her existence. Was she getting paranoid?

She unglued herself from the car seat, told Amir he could go home now—his motorcycle was parked in her garage and the Toyota was left with her overnight—and went over to Joel's house. She needed to talk to somebody.

Please, Joel, be home, she prayed, as she hurried down his driveway. She hadn't seen him for a week.

He was home, reading the *Indonesian Times* on the verandah, his feet up on the railing, a glass by his side. He looked very comfortable, and her stomach contracted. Oh, Joel, I love you, she said silently.

'Have a seat,' he invited, waving at a chair. 'Would you like a drink?'

'A double,' she said gloomily.

'Had a bad day?' He rose to his feet slowly, waiting for an answer.

'You could say that.'

'Do you want to talk about it?'

'Do you mind? I need to get something off my chest or I'll explode. You've no idea ... I'm so mad, I could. . . .'

He held up his hand. 'Wait, hang on a minute, let me get you that drink first. What do you want? The usual?'

'Yes, please. Thanks.'

Glass in hand, she began to tell him that people had been avoiding her, that she had known for a while that something was wrong. She told him what Josie had said. She sighed. 'I don't know why I can't just laugh about it. It's too petty for words. I mean, why do they even care about me? Don't they have worries of their own? God, I can't stand those *small* minds!' She raged on for a while longer and Joel just listened to her without interrupting.

When finally she was finished, he shook his head slowly, the gleam of humour in his eyes unmistakable.

Lauren groaned. 'Please, don't laugh!'

He laughed. 'Oh, Lauren, really, it's hilarious. I know you're mad as hell, but step back a little and see the situation for what it is. They're jealous of you, that whole bitchy batch of women.'

She stared at him. 'Josie said the same thing.'

'Josie isn't dumb.'

She sipped her drink. The air around them was oppressive. It hadn't rained for months and months and everything was drying up and shrivelling away. The sky was dark and heavy with clouds, but it had been like that for days and the rain did not come down.

'It's not easy when everybody treats you like a leper,' she said, feeling sorry for herself, 'even though they're wrong and malicious and hypocritical. I wouldn't want them for my friends if they tried.' She straightened in her chair. 'Anyway, I'll live. Who cares? I'll show them, those miserable witches!'

'Good for you!' Joel grinned, and reached for her glass. 'I'll pour you another one.'

Soon after that the phone rang—a call from Jakarta he'd been expecting, he said. Lauren finished her drink and left while he was still on the phone, waving her thanks through the window. He smiled and gave her the thumbs-up sign.

She tried hard to be cheerful, but life seemed to go steadily downhill from there. What she needed to lift her spirits was a love affair. But the man who featured in her romantic fantasies was being a good neighbour and showing no further inclinations to amorous intimacies. Maybe he needed a little push in the right direction. But she'd never done any active man-chasing and she wasn't too delighted at the idea of having to resort to that. It wasn't very good for her ego. Besides, Joel was perfectly capable of doing his own chasing if he felt so inclined.

Apparently he did not feel so inclined.

She had had a demonstration of the more passionate nature lurking under his cool exterior, but why wasn't he showing her more often?

Maybe he simply wasn't in love with her.

That idea didn't do her ego any good, either.

She kept thinking of the few times he had kissed her, reliving the moments. He had shown her then more of the real Joel than at any other time. He had tender feelings for her. Or was she just imagining things?

Patience wasn't one of Lauren's virtues, but she decided that instead of going after him with female tricks, which she didn't like anyway, she would try to improve her character by cultivating patience. When it came to female tricks she wasn't terribly practised and she had the idea that Joel would see through her in an instant, which would be humiliating, demoralising, and not good for her ego.

She seemed to be worrying a lot about her ego lately. By now she should have left the aches and pains of puberty way behind. Maybe it was all the stress and strain of being an outcast in the community. Try as she might, it wasn't easy to take.

She went on another trip, visiting more villages. It

was horrible. She hated it. It was the worst trip she'd made since coming to Indonesia—drought and poverty and women working for fifty cents a day.

She was sick for two days with some intestinal trouble, something picked up from the food, probably. She lay in a hot little hotel room, feeling wretched and very sorry for herself. She felt lonely and alone, although she had two other people with her who kept coming in and checking up on her anxiously, offering food and drinks, but all she wanted was to be left alone. She wanted Joel to appear magically in the doorway and sit down by her bed and hold her hand and promise her she wasn't dying.

She wasn't dying. She recovered, having lost a couple of pounds, by the looks of her hollow-eyed face in the mirror. She continued the trip, seeing more poverty and drought, and finding another factory where women worked for fifty cents a day. People hadn't been able to plant the rice because of the lack of irrigation water. Food was expensive. Even the goats were beginning to look scrawny. The heat was unbearable.

It was one misery after another, and by the time she came home she was so depressed she was ready to get on the next plane back to the States and forget everything, go to a four-star restaurant, drink champagne, spend five hundred dollars on luxuries at Lord and Taylor and pretend the world was a fine place to live in.

A long, cool bubble bath didn't help. Sitting in the living room, wrapped in a *kain*, Lauren contemplated her negative state of mind. She couldn't even shake her mood of doom and gloom when Joel arrived at the house unexpectedly. She told him about her trip, how depressed she was by what she had seen.

'Sometimes I just want to pack up and leave. I lie awake at night wondering and worrying and getting angrier and angrier because so little is done that really means anything. All the waste and corruption and politicking, it's so infuriating. . . .' She made a helpless gesture and sagged down in a chair like a sack of sand.

'Don't let it get to you too much,' he said calmly. 'It's counter-productive, you know that. There are a lot of bad things going on, there always have been, but try not to get too emotionally involved. It's not healthy. You have to build up some defences or you won't last.'

A sermon was not what she needed. She glared at him, feeling the anger rising in her. She jerked straight up in the chair. '*Healthy? Last?* Have you seen some of these people who've been around for twenty, thirty years? Have you ever listened to them talk? They're cynical and bitter or just don't give a damn. But they last, oh, yes, they last!' She paused to catch her breath.

He watched her, not batting an eyelid, making her angrier still.

'Well, let me tell you, Joel, I don't want to become like that, if that's what it takes to *last*! I don't want to be hard and uncaring and not feel anything when I see sick and hungry people who are too downtrodden to help themselves, and spout all those convenient reasons and excuses for why it's that way. Have you ever really listened to those long-timers? Oh, they're so smart! They've seen it all, they know it all, and the way they talk about the people makes me sick! *I* don't want to grow old like that! Losing my respect for people as human beings, talking about them as if they were some lower form of life!'

She was overreacting and over-generalising in a big way, but she couldn't help herself. For a calm-natured person, she was sure being emotional. Was she cracking up?

'I didn't say that's what you have to do,' he said, oh, so cool. 'All I said was that you need some defences. It doesn't mean you have to be hard and calloused and cynical.'

'It seems to go together! And I *do* have some

defences, a thin veneer maybe, but that's all right. I do fine for long periods of time. Then suddenly something happens, or maybe things have accumulated and reached saturation point, and the veneer cracks. In the end I patch it up and nothing much is lost. It's probably *healthy* to go through a spell like this now and then. It may not be a lot of fun, but for my emotional state it might not be so bad. It puts things back into perspective. I take stock of what I'm doing.'

She stopped, shifted in her chair, and let out a sigh.

Joel stretched his legs and folded his hands behind his head. 'And?'

Lauren shrugged, feeling deflated. 'It scares me. I spend a lot of time in the office, pushing paper, reading reports, designing pretty charts with pretty pictures, and having long discussions about theories and academic positions, and so on and so on. I start questioning myself. After all, what am *I* doing that's so earth-shaking? Nix!'

'You try.'

'Oh, yes, I try. But it's not enough. I've got to do better than that. You should have seen those women I saw this week!'

She stood up and wiped her forehead with the back of her hand. 'I'm so tired, I can't think. I'm sorry I unloaded on you like that. I didn't mean to bore you with my miseries.'

Joel came to his feet and stood before her. 'Lauren, don't be sorry. Talk to me any time you need to, please.' There was an odd note in his voice.

Her eyes filled with tears and she averted her face. His hands were on her shoulders, drawing her a little closer. Her throat ached, her mouth worked. She couldn't control the trembling of her body. She was going to shake into a thousand tiny fragments.

'Joel,' she whispered, 'hold me . . . please hold me.'

His arms slid around her back and he pulled her to

him. She buried her face in his neck. His breath fanned
her bare shoulder. Her body ached for him. Sweet
agony, sweet yearning. Oh, Joel, love me, say you love
me!

He lifted her face and kissed her with a sudden
unexpected fierceness, all composure gone. Clinging to
him, she took it, gave it back, her senses singing,
dancing, soaring.

Noise—footsteps outside. She felt him grow rigid.

'The *jaga*,' she whispered, 'just making his rounds.'
Like a bad movie, she thought. Phones ringing, people
knocking on doors, roofs crashing in at all the wrong
moments, breaking spells, spoiling intimacies.

Joel cursed under his breath. It made her laugh.

'What's so funny?' he asked.

'I've never heard you use that kind of language
before.'

'You haven't heard anything yet.' He took her hand
and led her out of the room with its bright light and
open windows, down the hall to her bedroom. He
opened the door, closed it, crossed to the window and
drew the curtains. He turned on the bedside lamp, sat
down next to her on the edge of the bed and took her
hand. They gazed at each other in silence. No
questions, no answers, no words at all. They had peace
and privacy and each other.

Still looking at each other, they began to touch,
fingers gently stroking, sliding over smooth skin and
angles and curves. He loosened her *kain* and it fell away
from her body. He smiled as his gaze travelled over her
and she didn't move. Shadows on the wall. Joel—large
and overpowering, she—smaller, hair falling forward
along her cheeks. His hand moved across the wall in
shadow and touched her breast. Shivering, she closed
her eyes.

They lay together on the bed, his bare body smooth
and firm against her. She put her arms around him,

clinging, clinging, filled with fear that he might get up and leave.

He didn't.

Was this one of her fantasies? No, no, no . . . it was real, so real, so familiar and wonderful and joyous. Better than any fantasy, this.

'Open your eyes,' he whispered.

She did, seeing her own feelings of rapture reflected in his eyes, seeing love. Had they been here before? They knew each other so well in this land of pleasure and delight—knowing how to please with intimate familiarity. Their bodies were tuned in to each other, belonged together. Oh, Joel, she thought, I knew, I knew!

Closing his eyes, he muttered something, pressing her hard against him. Nothing left now of the cool, composed man, so fully in control most of the time. No control now. Thought and reason abandoned, there was only the taste and touch and smell of each other. Senses soaring, they drowned in each other.

He kept on holding her. Sweet languor, soft murmurings, gentle caresses. Tender kisses on her eyes, her mouth, her hair. She opened her eyes and he was there, seeing her, knowing her. They smiled at each other in silence.

They fell asleep, holding tight.

Surfacing from deep, peaceful sleep, Lauren found him gone the next morning. Disappointment rushed through her, then anger at his sneaking away like a thief in the night. Making love and not waking up together was no good. *No good!* she thought furiously, kicking off the sheet and jumping out of bed. Her eye caught the clock. Seven thirty-five. Oh, good lord, she should have been at the office five minutes ago! She raced through the shower, dressed, ate on the run and dashed out of the door. Amir was leaning lazily against the Toyota, by all appearances perfectly prepared to wait for her until Doomsday if necessary.

The office reeked of stale cigarette smoke, fresh cigarette smoke, bad coffee, and Brut. Ed sat at his desk, smoking and staring into space, two dozen hairs carefully arranged over his bald spot.

'Are you in the middle of your morning meditation, or can we talk?' asked Lauren as she approached his desk.

He took a minute to focus his eyes. 'I never meditate. Vodka works for me.' Pushing back his chair, he put both his feet on top of his desk and made himself comfortable. 'Tell me, how was your trip?'

'It was a bummer. I hated it. And I want you to know that I'm going to say so in my report. No flowery cover-ups. No diplomatic gobbledygook. No politicking. I'm not going to worry about anybody's tender toes—I'm going to say exactly what I mean. You should have seen some of the things I saw this week! I. . . .'

'Sit down, kid, and tell me all about it.'

Oh, how she hated his patronising manner! Sit down, kid, and tell Daddy all your troubles. Daddy will take care of everything. Don't you worry your pretty little head about it. What did he think she was doing here? Playing little kids' games?

Glaring at him, she sat down. 'I'm sick and tired of going on these trips and visiting these factories where women work their fingers to the bone for a pittance. Factories full of *women*. Where are the men?'

Well, she knew where the men were. They were working their fingers to the bone doing other kinds of work, but generally speaking earning more, even if that still was pitifully little.

She should have known better than to start an argument about that with Ed. In no time they were involved in a raging verbal battle.

The day promised nothing good.

Her fury unleashed, she went back to her desk and began to write her report. Ed wasn't going to like it. He'd probably make her rewrite it. His major effort in life seemed to be directed towards keeping everybody happy at any price. No trouble, please. Life is too short. Fix it up, kid, this is no good. She could hear him say it already. To hell with him! She banged away at the rotten little typewriter as if it would help her get rid of her frustrations.

Half a year to go. Six months. A thought occurred to her, and she stopped typing and turned around in her chair.

'Ed, did my contract come while I was gone?'

'Contract?' Ed looked blank. He was good at that.

Lauren sighed. 'I told you about it. They couldn't give me a contract for the whole year for some bureaucratic reason. They gave me one for six months and assured me the renewal for the rest of the year would be automatic. Coleman said he'd get it signed and sent off from Jakarta before he went back to the States. It should be here by now.' She frowned. 'I talked to Coleman on the phone last week.'

'I didn't see it.'

'Did you get a telex, a phone call, something?'

'No, not about that. I got a telex with the football scores and one to say that Coleman's replacement has arrived. Adams is his name—Fred Adams.'

'I know. Oh, damn! If I don't get that contract I'm in trouble. My time is up on Tuesday.'

'It'll probably get here today or Monday.' Ed searched busily for his cigarettes, looking under stacks of paper in his desk, opening drawers, checking the breast pocket of his pink shirt.

'It's on the floor,' she said, seeing the package next to his desk. It was touching how she had his undivided attention. She watched as he extracted a cigarette from the package and lighted it. 'I'm going to call Jakarta and see,' she announced.

He blew out a cloud of smoke. 'Sure, good idea.'

She'd do it at home that afternoon. There was a three-minute limit on long-distance phone calls made from the office, and there was nothing more irritating than to be cut off in the middle of a conversation. To spare herself the aggravation, she used her home phone and kept track of her business calls on a piece of paper.

She worked steadily for several hours until her empty stomach began asking for food. Having left in a hurry that morning, she had brought no lunch. Amir went out to find her something to eat and returned with some skewered goat meat and something ricy wrapped in banana leaves. Lauren's report was almost finished and she didn't want to go out and lose momentum. When it was done she took it to the secretary and asked her to type up the finished copy. Lauren didn't show the draft to Ed. He was going to have to take it the way she had written it.

On the way home she stopped at Galael's to do some shopping—bread, eggs, soda water, soap. On impulse she bought a big Tobler chocolate bar with almonds. She deserved a treat.

She thought of Joel. She'd been quite successful all morning in pushing thoughts of him to the background, but memories came rushing back now. Oh, Joel, I love you, she thought. Maybe the world was not such a bad place after all. At least not for her this very moment.

The green bean tree (she still called it by that name) had never looked more beautiful with its fiery red blooms. Even the heavy clouds were beautiful with their promise of rain. The house shone with cleanliness and somehow did not seem so bare. Yanti had cut off some of the orchids growing on the verandah and put them in a jar on the coffee table. The ice water she drank even tasted wonderful, like spring water, which it wasn't.

Then she remembered the phone call. She dialled Jakarta and managed to get through right away. Mr Adams was out to lunch, she was told. At three o'clock in the afternoon? Most likely he wasn't eating anything out of a banana leaf. Most likely he wouldn't be returning to his office. She told the secretary it was an urgent matter and could she call him at home? Could he call her back? She gave the woman her number.

As she turned around she found Joel standing in the open door.

'*Selamat sore,*' he said, smiling.

Her body grew warm at the sight of him. 'Hi.' She wanted to fly in his arms, but her legs felt curiously unsteady. Looking at him now, she had never been more certain that he was hers, and only hers.

He had to know it too, feel it, like she felt it. Last night he must have felt the sense of communion, the togetherness, the intimate familiarity of their love-making. There had been nothing strange or awkward about it. They were made for each other. Her eyes wouldn't leave his face. She felt transfixed. Say something, she thought. Tell me you love me.

'My gas tank is empty,' he said, 'and my spare is empty as well, because I forgot to call for a new one.'

Lauren stared at him. 'What?' she asked numbly.

'My gas tank is empty. Could I have your spare one? I'll get us two full ones delivered tomorrow.'

It took all her strength to pull herself together. 'Of course. It's in the garage.' She walked to the door, her legs wooden, her heart cold. How dared he do this to her? He'd spent the night with her and he acted as if nothing had happened. A one-night stand, was that all it meant to him? Nice while it lasted. Finished and forgotten the next day. Business as usual. *You insensitive clod!* she wanted to scream at him.

'Over there,' she said icily, pointing at the blue tank.

He looked at her in quick appraisal, raising his

eyebrows in surprise. 'What's the matter with you?' he asked.

'Men!' she spat. 'Sometimes I really *hate* men! Last night you were making *love* to me. Now you walk in and talk about a goddamned *gas tank*! Well, there it is! Take it!' Whirling around, she stormed towards the door, but not fast enough. Joel clamped his hands on her shoulders, turned her, pushed her to the wall, pressed his body intimately against hers, and kissed her.

Oh, boy, did she get kissed! By the time he had finished with her she felt thoroughly ravished.

He looked very satisfied with himself. 'Was that what you had in mind?'

'You're an animal,' she uttered breathlessly.

'At your service.' He grinned wolfishly. 'Blind, naked passion, wasn't that what you wanted? Normally I keep myself under control in the middle of the day in front of servants sweeping floors and drivers washing cars and gardeners watering flowers.' He made a sweeping gesture encompassing the general surroundings of house and yard.

'You could have *said* something. You didn't have to come barging in here like any old businessman off the street trying to make a deal. I have feelings!'

'So I noticed,' he commented dryly, and she shot him a vicious look that made him burst into laughter.

'Don't you laugh at me!' She was beginning to feel very foolish. Why was she overreacting to such a ridiculous extreme? Why was she being too over-sensitive? Had he really done anything that justified such an outburst of emotion?

'Why shouldn't I laugh?' he asked, drawing her into his arms again. 'You're funny. You surprise me.'

What was she supposed to say to that? She surprised him—she bet she did! She surprised herself, too. She sighed, and he grinned down into her face.

'I'm sorry, I guess I'm an insensitive boor.' He

brushed his lips against hers. 'Last night was special. I didn't say it, but I knew it and I felt it. This morning I hated to leave you and I thought of waking you up, but that seemed such a selfish thing to do. You'd had such a hard day and you were sleeping so peacefully, so I just slipped out.'

Her anger had melted away. She wound her arms around his neck, feeling soft and tender feelings returning. 'I'm sorry I was such a witch.'

'Witches are my favourite people,' he said. 'They never bore me.'

'Joel,' she whispered, 'will you stay with me tonight again?'

He shook his head regretfully. 'I can't. I have to take some people from Jakarta to dinner and I'm afraid it might get late tonight. I'm sorry.' He kissed her lightly.

She wished she hadn't asked. Talk about romance! Here she was, propositioning a man in a garage lit by a glaring fluorescent tube and smelling of gasolene and cardboard, while her legs were being chewed up by a swarm of mosquitoes.

'How about some tea instead?' she suggested.

Joel threw his head back and laughed. 'Terrible second choice, but I'll take it.'

'You like Tobler's chocolate?'

He considered that, face solemn. 'What kind?'

'Bittersweet with almonds.'

'My absolute favourite.'

They left the garage, laughing like children, forgetting the gas tank.

Lauren's mouth was full of chocolate when the phone rang. She took a gulp of tea and swallowed hastily.

Fred Adams on the line, returning her call. He had a slight Southern drawl, irritating. He called her ma'am. She didn't like the tone of his voice.

'Mr Adams,' she began, 'I'd like to know what's happening with my contract. Mr Coleman told me it would be signed and in the mail last Monday. I still don't have it and my present contract runs out on Tuesday.'

'I'm aware of the problem, ma'am. I was going to call you about it today, but something intervened. I'm afraid your contract will not be renewed.'

Her heart dropped into her shoes, her breath stuck in her throat. Something was wrong.

'I'm sorry, I don't understand. There must be a mistake.'

'No, ma'am, no mistake. I just came in from Washington with the word. I'm sorry.'

He didn't sound sorry in the least.

'Mr Adams,' she said with a note of desperation, 'it was supposed to have been signed by the old project manager, Mr Coleman, the man you replaced. He didn't tell me there was any problem. The job was going well, everything was fine. So what *is* this? Would you tell me that, please?'

'Ma'am, the problem is that your contract cannot be renewed owing to budget shortages and changing priorities.'

'They can't do this to me! They wanted me to do this job for a year! My contract was to be renewed as a matter of course!'

'I'm sorry, ma'am. If there's anything we can do. . . .'

Sure, sure, she thought bitterly, slamming the phone down. She was shaking all over. Her face felt drained of colour. She turned and staggered back to her chair, and eyed her cold tea in revulsion. She glanced at Joel, who was leafing absentmindedly through a magazine.

'Did you hear that?' she asked. 'Did you *hear* that? The bastards! They're not renewing my contract! I've got to go home!'

Joel put the magazine down. 'I'm sorry. I take it you weren't expecting that piece of news.'

She got out of her chair. She couldn't sit still, her

body was twitching with rage. 'No! They kept telling me how good a job I was doing! Everything was fine—no problems! Contract would be signed and in the mail. Coleman *told* me that! Now they have a new project manager in Jakarta, fresh from Washington, complete with Southern drawl and yes ma'am, no ma'am, sorry ma'am every other word. Oh, I could scream!'

Instead she leaned her forehead against the wall and pounded her fists. It had happened to other people, she knew. A consultant's nightmare. Part of the game.

'They could have given me some warning! Oh, no, they wait till I have two days left and dump the news on me. Two days! Two days to get packed up and ready to leave. I'll have to travel on my own time. They won't pay me for that. I wonder if they have my tickets yet. Probably couldn't get me a flight until the end of the week.' She raged on, pounding the wall with her fists in frustration.

But it wasn't the loss of time and money that upset her most, not even the unfairness of it all, of being treated like a piece of luggage, a pawn in somebody else's chess game. It was the knowledge that she'd have to leave Joel.

Without an income she couldn't stay around. No work, no money, no house. Going home was the only thing she could do. Look for another job. If she were lucky she'd end up in Chad or Pakistan for a few months. If she weren't lucky she'd have to sit around Barbara's Bethesda apartment and watch soap operas on TV, chewing celery as she watched her savings dwindle away. No Joel. How could she possibly live without Joel?

He had come up behind her, was taking her fists away from the wall, and drew her to him, his arms around her waist. She leaned back against him, needing his strength, his comfort. Anger ebbed away and depression settled in. There was always an end to everything. She'd done this before, leaving a man and ending a relationship, but it had never really hurt. This time it felt like the end of the world. Joel was different, Joel was special, Joel was hers. They were connected by invisible bonds and they shouldn't be separated.

She turned in his arms, tears flooding her eyes. 'I don't want to leave you,' she whispered.

'We have a few more days.'

It wasn't what she wanted to hear. She didn't want a few more days, it wasn't enough. She wanted more from him, but he was silent. Maybe this was not the time.

Finally she disengaged herself. She picked up her tea-cup, dumped the contents into a potted palm and poured another cup from the pot. Her hands were sore from pounding the wall. What a ridiculous, melo-dramatic thing to do!

'The English say tea cures everything,' she said doubtfully. 'Let's see what it'll do for me.'

'You might be better off with a glass of brandy or whisky,' Joel said dryly, dumping his own cold tea in the plant pot. Maybe it would do the palm some good. It didn't look too grand with its dried-up leaf tips. Tea, her grandmother used to say, is good for plants. She'd always give left-over tea to her plants and they flourished.

So what was she thinking about in the middle of a crisis? Plants and tea. It would make more sense to think about her work that nobody was going to finish now. The project was cancelled, she was cancelled, the women working for fifty cents a day were cancelled. That Fred Adams and his bosses probably hated women, were male chauvinists of the worst sort. Women weren't important and certainly not the kind that made fifty cents a day. Changing priorities, he'd said. Whose priorities? She'd give a good sum to find out. They probably wanted to spend the money on something more visible, something you could put a plaque on: *Given to the People of Indonesia by the People of the United States of America.* Or maybe some academician in the higher echelon of the bureaucracy liked research, tons of paper, lots of print. Stacks of reports and studies and statistics nobody would read or use.

'Do you know how I feel?' she demanded.

'I can guess.'

'I feel insulted, humiliated!'

'You weren't fired, Lauren,' he pointed out.

'I wasn't? It sure feels like it was! It comes down to the same thing.' She replaced her half-full cup of tea back on its saucer. Tea didn't do it for her. She got up and went to the bar. 'I think I'll have that drink. It's early, but what the heck. Would you like one?'

Somehow, during the next hour, she collected herself, assembling the wreckage of her emotions and smiling bravely as she said goodbye to Joel when he left to entertain the people from Jakarta.

The clouds had never seemed darker, the air never more humid and oppressive. Please, God, let's have some rain.

Alone in the empty house, she watched and listened. Dark clouds glowered above, lightning slashed the sky, rolling thunder growled through the heavens. Then rain hurled itself to earth, smashing into vegetation and pavements, churning and swirling down streets and gutters. The smell of wet dust and dirt rose in the steaming air.

It was glorious! With her legs tucked under her, Lauren sat in front of the open window, enjoying the spectacle. When the worst was over and the rain calmed down into a calm, steady soaker, she moved to the verandah. For a long time she just sat there, not tired, just staring off into the dark wet world.

She couldn't sleep that night. Finally, at five-thirty,

she got up, made some tea and sat on the verandah to watch the sunrise. Sipping her tea, she listened to the early morning sounds of birds and chickens, and watched the subtle change of colours as the sun rose above the horizon. Everything was wet and gleaming. At some time in the night the rain had stopped, but puddles and muddy roads were left behind everywhere. The world seemed clean and green, revived already. Plants and trees and flowers were almost visibly soaking up the moisture and readying themselves for new growth.

At home in the States it was winter now. November—cold, rainy, windy. The leaves had turned and fallen, leaving the trees bare and grey. She didn't want to go back. She didn't want to leave Joel. Something had to happen, some miracle, some divine intervention.

But nothing happened. Nothing.

Joel helped her pack. He was silent, withdrawn, alien. Lauren wanted him to put his arms around her, hold her, make love to her, but he didn't. At the end of an endless Saturday she could take no more. This was her last night here. Tomorrow she'd fly to Jakarta and on Monday she'd get her plane tickets at the office and leave Indonesia.

'Please,' she said, putting her head on his shoulder, 'I can't stand you being so quiet. Say something. Talk to me.'

He stayed with her that night. They clung together in the dark, making love, desperately, sadly. Everything was wrong. There was no joy, no happiness.

A terrible farewell.

CHAPTER SEVEN

TOKYO Airport. Lauren was waiting for her flight to New York. She felt reasonably rested. As she had flown in from Jakarta the day before, the airline had generously allowed one night in Japan. She had slept deeply and dreamlessly for the first time in days in a clean, cool room at the Narita View Hotel.

All through the flight from Jakarta her throat had ached and her eyes had burned. She'd been determined not to break down in tears amid an odd assortment of strangers in an aeroplane. It had not been easy. Oh, Joel, she kept thinking, why did you let me go?

She was calm now. Inside her nothing moved. There was a stillness and a silence, a strange absence of emotion. She felt nothing. Some sort of defence mechanism had activated itself, for which she was grateful. It wouldn't do to fall to pieces in a country where no one knew her. In the last few days she had spent so much mental energy on emotional issues that she was worn out. She needed a reprieve and she was getting it.

She made her mind a blank, giving her thoughts a rest. She gazed at the people around her, from all corners of the world and in all manner of dress. She sighed and stretched her legs. Not too much longer before her flight would be called.

Goodbye, Far East, goodbye, Joel.

There was a faint ringing noise. Ambulance? Fire truck? No. It was inside the building somewhere, but she couldn't locate the source. It grew louder and louder, a high-pitched sound that seemed to fill the air. She looked around in alarm. No one seemed to notice.

Facial expressions had not changed—they were as bored, impatient or blank as before. Was she the only one hearing it? She covered her ears with her hands.

The sound was coming from inside her.

Taking a deep breath, she tried to calm herself. Then, to her utter relief, the ringing began to fade away. She lowered her hands, noticing people's curious stares. She became aware of a strange sense of weightlessness, as if she were suddenly floating above the ground, light as a cloud. It was a glorious feeling, so free, so joyous. She had no fear at all. The air was filled with radiant colours, clear and brilliant hues she had never seen before. They wavered and shimmered around her as she floated through space. She'd never seen anything more beautiful, never experienced anything so peaceful and soothing.

She sighed and blinked her eyes. Around her the airport terminal began to vibrate. Furniture, luggage, telephone booths, everything was moving and shifting. Shapes and forms grew hazy. People and noises faded. The waiting area slowly changed, growing smaller and darker. . . .

The room she was in was very dark, with big pieces of carved furniture, heavy red draperies, and a marble floor covered with Oriental rugs. She could see the design of the carpets very clearly, notice the intricacies of the carved furniture. There was great familiarity in the things around her—this was her house. Her dress was very long and black and voluminous. Inside her everything was as dark as the room, as black as her dress. Through a crack in the closed curtains sunlight filtered into the room. She opened the door and walked outside into the courtyard with its potted plants, its glittering fountain and the statue of the Virgin Mary. Through an archway she went into the gardens full of flowering bushes, roses in many colours, blossoming trees. Oh, it was lovely here with the birds chirping and

the butterflies fluttering and the bees buzzing around
the flowers, but the loveliness of it all did not touch her
and with her eyes cast down she walked on the pebbled
path towards the roses.

With her gloved hand she broke off a big yellow rose
and a thorn pierced her glove and pricked her finger.
She took off the black glove and examined her finger,
seeing a bright red drop of blood. Putting her finger in
her mouth, she noticed the irony taste of blood on her
tongue.

She continued down the path. At the end stood the
small chapel surrounded by tall trees, but she did not go
in. Walking past and beyond the chapel, she went to the
small graveyard shaded by orange trees and knelt down
by one of the graves, putting down the rose. Without
words she prayed, a giving over of silent grief. The pain
twisted and churned inside her and tears pressed behind
closed lids. Would the tears never end? A memory
flickered and in her mind she saw the man who was no
longer with her. Smiling, laughing, he mounted a horse
and galloped off, waving at her. It was the last time she
had seen him alive and the image of his laughing face
haunted her.

Only memories were left, and the stone with his name
carved on it, and the dates: 1854–1885.

Slowly she came back to her feet, walked back to the
chapel and went in. It was dark and damp inside. She lit
a candle and knelt and prayed once again. There was
the smell of old wood, dust, dampness and candle wax.
She prayed for a long time. When she walked out of the
chapel into the sunlight, she felt a measure of peace.
Her knees ached from kneeling on the cold floor.

The light began to fade as she walked back to the
house. Shapes and colours of trees and flowers seemed
to dissolve in the air. She couldn't see the house any
more, and at her feet the gravelled path had vanished.

Noises penetrated her consciousness. There were

people again, and voices talking and bright electric
lights. Tokyo Airport.

Lauren glanced at the clock. Only seconds had
passed, but it felt as if she'd been gone for hours, had
come back from another time, another place. No
daydream, this, but a vision of herself in full colour and
detail in another century. She had heard, seen, smelled
and tasted with real-life clarity. She could recall every
detail of it—see the designs on the rugs, hear the insects
in the garden, taste her blood, smell the candle wax, feel
the agonising sorrow.

The place had been Spain.

And the man had been Joel.

Days later as she sat in Barbara's apartment in
borrowed sweater and slacks (her winter clothes reeked
of mothballs and were at the cleaner's), the vision was
still as clear and vivid as a movie. No dream or fantasy
had ever had this clarity and realism. Dreams faded and
didn't have this Technicolor detail. It had been as
clear as anything in the room she was in now—the feel
of her clothes, the smell of freshly brewed coffee, the
pattern of the sofa upholstery. She could still recall the
carving on the furniture in that other room, the sting of
the rose thorn as it pricked her finger, the smell of the
dampness in the chapel.

The beautiful Spanish house with its courtyard and
its lovely garden was intimately familiar. The laughing
man on the horse. . . . The melancholy sadness and the
sense of loss she had felt all through her life seemed no
longer strange. Had she grieved, all that time, for the
death of a lover, a husband?

Maybe we've met in another life. Joel's facetious
suggestion came suddenly back to her.

Reincarnation.

She didn't believe it. There was no such thing. Her
mind was playing tricks with her. She was imagining

things. There had to be an explanation for the things that she saw and felt and experienced. Something logical and rational. One day she would understand it all and laugh about her wild ideas.

Maybe.

She turned on the television. A handsome man was brushing his teeth with Colgate. A towel was wrapped around part of his anatomy, but a broad, bare chest covered with dark curly hair was displayed for everyone to see. Gorgeous specimen. Dark eyes, magnificent teeth (of course) and a dazzling smile. He was followed by a housewife in pressed slacks and neatly buttoned blouse and combed hair (who did she think she was kidding?) busy throwing dirty socks in the washing machine, smiling confidently. The socks came out clean.

This was life—brushing teeth and washing socks. And being out of work. Lauren groaned. Not a cell in her body showed any enthusiasm to go back to work. She had no desire at all to get back on a plane, to go to another strange place, an empty house, new people. She was so tired, felt such a weariness of the spirit.

Her life had too many silent spaces. She had filled her years with passing friendships, ever-changing jobs, endless travel—experiences valuable in many ways, but making her life rootless and fleeting and lonely. She seemed to be adrift in time, with nothing and no one to hold on to.

She longed for some permanence, some stability, a man in her life who would not go away and whom she would not leave. A life together. Joel was lonely too. Why then were they so far apart?

It was too close to the holidays to get a new assignment; she'd go back to work in January. She'd spend Christmas with her parents in Iowa—a white Christmas maybe. A turkey dinner with cranberry sauce and pumpkin pie and eggnog and homemade cookies. She'd have to forget Joel, forget everything, start over.

She couldn't forget Joel. He was part of her, and in some strange way he had been with her all her life. He belonged with her. Every night she dreamed of him, and pain churned in her like a living thing.

Barbara was not to be fooled. She was sharp, observant and had X-ray vision. Barbara had her figured out within half an hour of her arrival.

'Tell me,' she said matter-of-factly, 'what is it? Anaemia, parasites, burn-out, or a man?'

Lauren told her everything—even about the strange experience she had had in Tokyo Airport. She wanted Barbara to laugh at her, so she could laugh at herself too. It would make all of it a joke. Barbara would have the perfect, logical explanation—something to do with flying, the Japanese air, or something in the food. Maybe everybody suffered from visions in Tokyo Airport.

Barbara did not laugh. She was fascinated and could barely contain her excitement. She got up out of her chair, blue eyes shining. 'It's fantastic! I can't believe it! You had a vision! An honest-to-God *remembrance!*'

Lauren stared at her. 'I thought you'd say I'm crazy.'

'Are you kidding? Of course not! You're one of the saner people I know.' She took a deep breath. 'Lauren, do you realise what that vision was? What it meant? Do you know why you thought you'd met Joel before?'

She shrugged. 'You tell me.'

'You've known each other in another life! You saw part of it in that vision. You know, I've read about this sort of thing. It happens more often than you think, but people don't like to talk about it, because people who haven't experienced it think you're crazy.'

Lauren could understand why. Barbara's reaction surprised her. 'I thought you'd have a logical explanation for it,' she said. 'Something to do with a chemical imbalance in my brain cells or something.'

'I'm *giving* you a perfectly good explanation.

Barbara embarked upon the subject of reincarnation with an enthusiasm that left Lauren open-mouthed. According to Barbara, Joel and she had had a love relationship in a previous existence and their souls had searched each other out again in this life. The music Joel had composed and which, inexplicably, Lauren had known for many years, was music from that other life. It had carried over in their consciousness because it had held special significance for them. At least, that was what Barbara believed.

'You're not serious,' said Lauren. 'You don't really believe all that?'

Barbara was unperturbed. 'Of course I believe it.'

'You, of all people . . . I hadn't expected it.'

'What do you mean, *me* of all people?'

'You're such a practical, rational person. You teach *chemistry*, for heaven's sake! I didn't think you'd go for all this unscientific, unsubstantiated stuff.'

'Lauren, there are a lot of things happening that people don't understand—E.S.P., poltergeists, all kinds of paranormal psychic phenomena. Just because we don't understand it doesn't mean it doesn't exist or that it isn't real. Did you know that secretly some police departments make use of psychics in difficult cases? *Secretly*, of course, because people wouldn't like the idea of the police dabbling in the paranormal.'

Lauren was silent. Of course she had heard about psychics finding lost children after everyone else had given up. She remembered reading something about aurology and the fact that certain individuals were able to detect different colours around people's bodies and deduce from that the state of their physical and emotional health. She'd seen a picture of a hand and its aura, taken by a camera with special film. She'd heard of out-of-body experiences, telepathy, and other strange things. She'd picked up a bit here and a bit there, never taking it very seriously, never giving it much thought.

She liked things concrete and verifiable and none of this was.

And much about my relationship with Joel isn't either, she couldn't help thinking.

From the very beginning there had been something mysterious between them. Her feelings for him, her ideas about having known him before, about having been together in Spain, all that was strange. And what about the music he had composed, the music she had known all her life? Where were all the explanations? She'd had a vision. Not a dream, not a drug-induced hallucination. It had appeared in the middle of a busy airport in clear electric light while she had been quietly waiting for a plane. She'd been perfectly calm and composed and in a sane state of mind.

'Since when have you been interested in parapsychology and reincarnation? You never mentioned it when I was here in the spring.'

'I met someone soon after you left.' Barbara grinned. 'Male, handsome, sexy eyes. Also very smart. He's a psychologist interested in paranormal phenomena. He's been involved with several research programmes. He got me interested. I started reading books about it, tried to find out more. It's fascinating, really.'

Lauren didn't know what to say. She didn't know what to believe. Her reason and logic were being assaulted from various directions and her mind was spinning in confusion.

'Just remember, Lauren, that when Galileo said the world was round, nobody believed him.' Barbara untangled her legs and rose to her feet. 'Come on, let's send out for a pizza.'

A couple of days later Lauren found a picture among her papers. It was a snapshot of one of the Monday Hashes. Hashers, dogs, children all milling about the *Anker Bir* truck. Everybody with wet clothes, sweaty faces, laughing mouths—a picture full of fun and silliness, with Joel right in the middle of it. Tears burned behind her eyes. She felt such a heaviness, such a weight in her chest and stomach and legs. . . . How could she ever live with only a memory of Joel?

He was on her mind all the time.

'What's going to happen?' she asked Barbara. 'If, according to you, we met because we were meant to be together, why aren't we together now? Why is he on the other side of the globe while I'm here? It doesn't make a lot of sense, does it?'

Barbara grimaced. 'I'm not a psychic, Lauren. I can only guess.'

'So guess!' A guess was better than nothing. She took a sip from her wine.

'He'll come looking for you again.'

Lauren groaned. 'Fairy tales always sound so nice. And we'll live happily ever after?'

'What do you want me to do? Look in a crystal ball? Read tea-leaves? Get a deck of tarot cards?'

'You believe in that hocus-pocus too?'

'I don't know yet; I haven't researched it.' Barbara gave a broad grin. She had beautiful teeth. 'It's my project for next year.' She finished her wine and poured some more for both of them.

Lauren sighed. 'So you think he'll come looking for me? I'd hate to think I'd have to reincarnate all over again just to see him again. It gets tiring, I can tell you.'

'There's a theory,' said Barbara, staring thoughtfully into her glass, 'that you're born again to finish what didn't get finished in your previous life.'

'Well, we certainly didn't finish anything in Indonesia!'

'It isn't over yet.' Barbara seemed very sure of herself. 'I told you, I think he'll be back.'

'When?'

'There you go again! How am I supposed to know?

Okay, okay, let me see.' She arranged herself comfortably, closed her eyes, and put on a mysterious expression. Silence. Lauren watched her. Was she meditating? Communicating with the gods? Calling on the spirits? Had she fallen asleep?

'When?' Lauren repeated after a while.

Barbara opened her eyes. 'Soon. Definitely very soon.'

'What is *soon?* Two days? Two months? Two years?'

Barbara shook her head. 'That I cannot tell. I'm not that good an oracle.'

'You can say that again! You're no help at all.' Lauren looked morosely into her empty glass.

'Have some more wine.' Barbara filled their glasses for the third time. 'Tell me again about your vision.'

Why not? What did it matter?'

Barbara nodded gravely as Lauren finished her tale. 'Apparently your love affair ended prematurely. Very tragic. You were probably married.' She contemplated her wine. 'The dates on the gravestone said he was thirty-one years old when he died. A little young to check out, I would think. Poor devil. Actually, he wasn't so poor as far as money was concerned, right?'

'The house was enormous, with fancy furniture and Oriental carpets, and it had a beautiful flower garden all around it.'

'And its own chapel and graveyard.'

'Yes.'

Barbara twisted excitedly in her chair. 'An estate! Oh, how romantic! Maybe he was a winegrower, or whatever you call these people. Sherry, of course, the very best.'

Lauren sipped her wine and nodded. She liked the idea.

'You said that in your thoughts you saw him ride away on a horse and that it was the last time you saw him alive. How did he die?'

'I don't know.' She frowned. 'I can't remember. I didn't think about it, I suppose. I remember just thinking that he was dead.'

'Maybe he fell off his horse and broke his neck. Or maybe somebody shot him. They had family feuds, blood feuds in those days, I think.' Barbara began to laugh softly. 'Maybe he'd been gambling and had just discovered that he was bankrupt and he hanged himself.'

'You're morbid!' With that kind of imagination she should be writing gory novels. But Lauren couldn't keep her face straight and grinned. 'Oh, Barbara, this is ridiculous!'

'It's fun!'

'Let's tear apart *your* love from another life! Do you know about any?'

Barbara grimaced. 'No. I try to have visions, but it won't work. I'd love to find out about myself. I've considered hypnosis, past life regression, that sort of thing. I saw it done on TV—fascinating!' She sighed dreamily, stretching lazily on the couch. 'Imagine, I might have been an Indian princess, or Queen Victoria's chambermaid, or a cloth weaver in ancient Egypt.'

'Or a dog—a Pekingese.'

Barbara gave her such a disgusted look that Lauren broke out laughing.

'No animals,' said Barbara.

'Who says?'

'Animals don't have souls.'

'Don't say that to a dog- or a cat-lover. Or to the animists of this world.'

'Okay, I won't.' She poured more wine, caught Lauren's eye and they both burst into laughter at the same time.

Lauren couldn't stop. She laughed until the tears poured down her face. And then it wasn't funny any more. Laughter changed into sobs. She leaned her head

on her arms on the coffee table and cried and cried.
And as it went on she felt a helpless rage build up.
Maybe it had been there all along and it was finally
coming to the surface. She lifted her head and clenched
her hands into fists.

'Why did he let me go?' she asked. 'If he loved me . .
why then did he?' She started pounding the coffee table
with her fists. 'He just let me leave, Barbara! He said
nothing! *Nothing!*' She kept on pounding the table like a
madwoman, then dropped her head back on her arms
and cried some more. There seemed to be no end to her
tears. Her whole body ached with the sobbing. The
memory burned in her mind.

Joel had taken her to the airport in Semarang, kissed
her goodbye and wished her good luck. During the
forty-five-minute flight to Jakarta in the delapidated F-
28 she had blindly stared out the window feeling cold
and hard like a statue, allowing herself no feelings and
no tears.

But the tears were catching up with her now.

Barbara put her arms around her. 'Everything will be
all right—I *know* it. Please, don't cry.'

Barbara wasn't laughing any more, either.

Two weeks later Lauren was still languishing on
Barbara's couch in front of the TV, watching soaps. No
Joel. No job. She'd had an offer for a two-month stint
in Benin and turned it down. She wasn't eating and she
wasn't sleeping and she had to do something.

'You'll have to do something,' said Barbara. 'You're
wading knee-deep in misery and you're fading before
my very eyes. Why don't you see a doctor?'

'I don't need a doctor.' She needed Joel.

'Like hell you don't! You're getting worse by the
day! There's no light and vitality in you. You hardly
eat. You lie awake. You look glassy-eyed. You act as if
somebody had died, for heaven's sake! You're so turned

into yourself you don't know whether I'm in the room or not. I go shopping, leaving you sitting there on the couch contemplating your toes, and two hours later I find you in the same position, looking vacant as a condemned building. Tell me, is that normal?'

Lauren shrugged. 'I don't know what a doctor could do for me.'

'Then maybe it's time you found out. Lauren, you look *awful*!'

Lauren glanced out the window. The first snow of the year was falling, big wet flakes that melted as soon as they hit the pavement. She should be delighted; as a child she had seen little snow, and it was magic, wondrous, delightful. But she felt nothing. In two weeks it would be Christmas. The city was ablaze with lights. Everything and the lamp-post was decorated. Everything sparkled and glowed and glittered. Christmas carols poured out of p.a. systems, filling the shopping malls and the department stores and spilling over into the streets. Colour and excitement everywhere. How she would have longed for this had she still been in Indonesia!

She looked away from the window and the falling snow. Barbara sat curled up in her chair, hugging a patchwork cushion and watching her anxiously. She might as well face it: it was no use sitting here in Bethesda hoping for Joel to appear. He wasn't going to. And she wasn't going to get another assignment until January. So why was she hanging around here?

'I'll go home for Christmas. I'll have my parents' doctor check me out.' She had no intention of doing that, but it would set Barbara's mind at ease.

Barbara seemed relieved, and Lauren felt guilty. She was a friend, and it hadn't been easy for Barbara to watch her steadily disintegrate on her couch. It was definitely time to take her miseries to her parents. Her mother would fix her chicken soup. It had always cured whatever ailed her. Maybe it would even cure a broken heart.

Barbara dropped her off at National Airport two days later. Lauren had managed to get a cancellation, which was good luck so close to the holidays. They hugged and kissed goodbye, and Lauren turned and walked into the building with her one suitcase. The rest of her belongings (summer clothes, mostly) were packed away at Barbara's place. Sooner or later she would leave for the tropics again and she would need her things again. Having a friend so close to Washington was a real convenience. Many of her colleagues spent their time in hotels.

The terminal was terribly crowded. The Christmas rush was on. Families with children were milling around everywhere—howling infants, nervous mothers, irritable fathers. There were the customary number of cool-looking businessmen with their tailored suits and shiny shoes and leather briefcases en route to New York or Philadelphia, hiding their faces behind the *Wall Street Journal*, the *Washington Post* or the *New York Times*.

So many people. So many faces. Strangers all.

No! She was seeing things.

It couldn't be!

She blinked, looked again. A man was coming towards her. It wasn't Joel; he just looked like him. Didn't he? Tall, dark. . . . She knew that walk, the set of the shoulders. Her heart began to thump and her knees wobbled as she moved forward. Was this an hallucination? She was in real trouble if she started imagining chance encounters in airports.

Joel, carrying a battered suitcase, coming towards her. Looking at her. Oh, God, it was him! It was him!

Somebody bumped into her.

'Hey, lady, look out where you're going!'

Lauren almost lost her balance and her suitcase slipped from her fingers and crashed to the floor. Her legs refused to move. Her feet seemed stuck in cement.

She had to hurry or she'd miss her plane. She still had to get her ticket at the counter, and the line was long. She glanced at the clock. She was going to miss her plane if she didn't move right now. She glanced back at the man. He was still there. It was Joel.

He stood in front of her. 'Lauren?' He dropped his suitcase at his feet.

She grinned stupidly. 'Joel?'

'We keep running into each other.' He was smiling, reaching out to her and taking her into his arms. It was an awkward embrace with all those layers of clothing between them—heavy sweaters and scarves and winter coats.

'Coincidence, do you think?' she murmured.

'Absolutely not.'

'Did you know I was here?' She was incredulous.

'No, but I was on my way to find you, on my way to Bethesda.'

'I was just leaving. How easily we could have missed each other!'

He shook his head and smiled. 'We were supposed to meet, don't you see? Fate, providence, whatever you want to call it.'

Her heart turned over. 'Predestiny.'

'Fine by me.' He lifted her chin and peered into her face. 'Have you been sick?'

'Yes,' she lied. 'I've had 'flu.' She could hardly tell him she'd been pining for him for the last several weeks.

'Let's get out of this hellhole.' He picked up his suitcase and took hers with his other hand, and marched to the exit. Lauren followed him in a trance, as if she were hypnotised and obeyed orders like a robot. The blast of cold air that hit them as they left the building sobered her up.

'Where are we going?' she asked.

'I've got a rental car. The rest is a surprise.' He grinned wolfishly. 'I'm going to abduct you, if you're willing.'

Was she willing? She'd go with him blindfolded and handcuffed, and like it.

'I have a reservation on a flight to Iowa,' she told him. 'My parents are expecting me. I'll need to phone them.'

'No problem. Let's get out of here first. We'll find a restaurant and you can call them from there.'

'I'd rather do it right now. They have to leave early to get to the airport to pick me up and I might miss them. There are phones right inside. I won't be long.'

'Okay, if you like. I'll hang on to your stuff.'

As Lauren went back inside, panic seized her. What if she went outside again and found him gone?

She had to wait for a few minutes before one of the phones was free, and it seemed an eternity. Please don't leave, she pleaded silently. Please be there when I get back. She heard her flight called. Too late now; she didn't have a ticket. Her suitcase was outside. If Joel wasn't there. . . . Her hands were clammy as she held on to the receiver. The phone rang and rang. Oh, God, they'd left for the airport already! Eager to pick her up, eager to see the beloved daughter. Guilt washed over her.

'Hello?'

Oh, blessed relief! 'Mom? This is Lauren. I'm at the airport, at National, but I'm not coming home. Not today, anyway. I . . . .' She didn't know what to say, what kind of reason or excuse to give her. She couldn't lie to her. She'd never been able to lie to her mother.

'Lauren, are you all right?'

'Oh, I'm fine, Mom! Finer than I've ever been. I met a friend just now, at the airport, by coincidence. A special friend. I can't leave now.' She was pleading. She felt guilty and helpless.

'What about Christmas?'

'I don't know yet. I'll call you. Please, Mom, don't be mad.'

She wasn't mad, she wouldn't be. She'd be disappointed. She'd been so delighted to hear Lauren was coming. It would be the first time in five years the whole family would be together at Christmas. Her sister and her husband and their two children would be there, and her brother and his wife and their new baby. She was supposed to be there too.

'Where will you be?' Her mother's voice was calm, and Lauren knew she was trying hard not to show her disappointment.

'I don't know yet. I'll call—I promise I'll call as soon as I get a chance.'

'Bring him home for Christmas. If he's that special, maybe he should be here, too.'

Lauren couldn't help laughing. 'Who said it was a man?'

Now her mother was laughing too. 'Come on, Lauren, I wasn't born yesterday. Of course it's a man!'

'Dad might not approve of him.'

'What's wrong with him?'

'He's not Navy.'

'Oh, your dad has mellowed in his old age. Don't worry about it.'

Lauren laughed. 'I wasn't.' She never had been. She remembered defying her father at seventeen by dating an enlisted man, a lowly sailor by the name of Sammy. Her father's anger had been frightening, but her need to rebel against him and the whole Naval way of life was stronger than her fear. She was supposed to associate only with young, promising officers, marry one and perpetuate the family tradition. Her independent nature rebelled against following a predetermined route. She wanted to do her own thing. So she had, and here she was, in love with a tropical marine biologist. At least, she thought dryly, he has something to do with water.

She promised once more to call as soon as she knew anything, then said goodbye, then she raced out of the building. Joel was standing exactly where she had left him, hands deep in his fleece-lined trench coat. The wind was blowing his hair around, flopping it over his forehead. He was the best-looking man in the world. Her heart was jumping for joy and she felt like dancing.

'What did they say?' he asked. 'Were they disappointed?'

'Of course. They want me there for Christmas. I promised to call later.'

He had rented a nice, comfortable Buick. Lauren thought of all the trips she had made in Indonesia in her Toyota Land Cruiser. Some difference.

Some difference in everything. She had never seen Joel wearing a sweater, and it looked cosy and comfortable.

'Tell me why you came for me,' she said as they left the city and drove west. 'Where are we going? What's happening?'

'Later,' he said. 'Right now I just want to drive for a while, be with you. Later we can talk.' He took her hand and squeezed it. He kept his eyes on the road as he spoke and returned his hand to the steering wheel. The traffic was bad. It was better to let him give his attention to the road.

Lauren was filled with exhilaration and she could barely sit still. Her thoughts ran amok. It was so good to be with him again.

'How's everybody in Semarang?' she asked for something to say.

He gave her a quick, sideways glance. 'The Furgesons are leaving next month.'

'Good riddance!'

'And Josie is pregnant. She's delirious with joy. Apparently they'd almost given up.'

'I'm glad for her. She'll be a good mother, our Josie.'

'And a new English couple just moved into your

house. He's an electrical engineer. Nice people. There's been quite a turnover in the last month. Lots of new faces around town, but I haven't met them all.'

They'd left the George Washington Parkway and were going through Virginia on route 7. Slowly, Lauren began to calm down. Slowly, her thoughts became less chaotic. Slowly, she was beginning to have doubts about this excursion.

What was this going to lead to? She remembered Joel when she had first met him, so cool towards her, so indifferent. Then there had been the gradual change in his behaviour, the casual conversations, the occasional smile. She remembered the times they had made love. And after all that he had just let her go. He had not tried to keep her with him. He had just let her leave. If he had loved her he would have said something.

How did it happen that she was in this car with him, not knowing anything? Not knowing where they were going or what he intended to do. Was he really just here to see her? Or was he planning to have Christmas with his family, thinking that a good time with her would fit in with it nicely? Maybe he was here on business. . . . Was she being naïve? After a few days of bliss he might just take off again. Thank you, Lauren, for the nice time. It had happened before; it might happen again—simple goodbye and good luck.

No, not again. She wasn't going through that agony again. She couldn't keep saying goodbye for ever.

She felt tight all over. Her hands lay clenched in her lap and her jaws were clamped shut. Surprised at the rigidity of her body, she tried to relax her muscles, but she didn't seem to be able to loosen them.

She was angry with herself. How could she have gone along with him as if she had no mind of her own, no rational thought at all? He walked into her life and she lost her common sense. She followed him out of the airport, floating on clouds, mindless as a rag doll.

And he, arrogant and presumptuous, hadn't even asked where she was going, whether she wanted to come with him. He had assumed she'd follow him, get in his car, go to the North Pole with him. Who did he think he was, that he could just commandeer her into this? She'd called off a trip home, all on a whim.

Where were they going?

'Is something wrong?' Joel asked suddenly. 'You're so quiet.'

Lauren took a deep breath. 'I'd like to know where we're going.'

'It's a surprise.' He glanced at her and frowned. 'Why are you so tense?'

'I'm wondering if I'm doing a stupid thing, going with you like this, on the spur of the moment. I didn't even stop to think.'

There was a pause. Her stomach turned itself into a knot. She glanced at his face. No expression. Eyes on the road, lines of strain around his mouth and eyes. He was tired.

'Lauren, I can't answer that for you. All I know is that I want to be with you. I want to talk to you, but not now, not here.'

It didn't help. She said nothing and gazed silently out of the window. The tension in the car was palpable. Well, what was it that she wanted from him? A contract in blood? *I, Joel Rockwell, promise to never leave you Lauren Carmichael.*

Yes, that was exactly what she wanted.

Clearly, she couldn't ask for that. Not here in a Buick going down route 7 in Virginia. There had to be a better place and a better time.

Joel had said he wanted to talk to her later. Okay, okay, she'd wait. Take her chances.

The air between them was heavy with unspoken thoughts. The silence screamed in her ears. Suddenly he began to slow down and pulled off the road.

Leaning his arms on the steering wheel, he stared straight ahead.

'Do you want me to turn back?' he asked.

'Joel, I didn't say that.'

'What do you want, then?'

'We'll leave it for later. You're right, this isn't the time or the place.'

'Lauren, I can feel your anger. You're radiating tension and I can't deal with it now. I'm tired. I flew in on the red-eye special from L.A. You know what that means.'

Yes, she knew what that meant.

'You shouldn't be driving,' she said.

His jaw tightened and his face grew into a stony mask. He opened his door, got out, slammed it shut, walked around to the passenger's side and pulled the door open.

'All right, you drive. Move over.' It was said in tightly controlled tones, but his whole body emanated cold anger.

Lauren slid behind the wheel, feeling afraid and angry and sorry that she'd said anything at all. She could have been more tactful.

But *he* could have been more explanatory! Why wasn't he telling her anything? Why were they having this ridiculous argument? Why all this tension? She probably wasn't any fitter to drive than he was.

'Where are we going?' she asked, her tone strangely husky. She switched on the engine and stared straight ahead. Her throat felt like sandpaper.

'Keep going straight on this road, past Leesburg, direction West Virginia. When you get to Harper's Ferry, wake me up.' He leaned his head against the back of the seat and closed his eyes, dismissing her.

Lauren hated him then. How dared he treat her like that! She was going to turn this vehicle around and head back to the airport. Maybe she could get another

flight to Iowa. She didn't care what he did with himself.
She didn't want any part of him ever again.

Her vision blurred.

Joel had come all the way from the other side of
the world to see her. Why was she questioning his
motives? What was the matter with her? She was
ruining something perfectly wonderful with her sus-
picious ideas. Her eyes burned. Why was she so
terrified?

Here they sat, illegally parked by the side of route 7
in Virginia, miserable. Well, *she* was miserable anyway.
Joel was asleep. In a minute they'd have a sheriff's car
with blue flashing lights checking up on them and
they'd end up with a ticket to round things off nicely.
She'd better get moving. She swallowed and blinked her
eyes in an effort to compose herself.

She eased the car into the flow of traffic and
continued towards West Virginia.

CHAPTER EIGHT

THE landscape looked dreary in the grey winter light.
The sky was heavy with clouds. Lauren hoped it
wouldn't rain, at least not until they'd reached their
destination, wherever that might be. Now and then she
glanced at Joel. He was fast asleep with his head resting
against the door, oblivious to everything. He seemed
more relaxed now, but the fatigue was still evident.

She thought about the endless plane trip, the
boredom, the plastic food, the hundreds of dollars he'd
spent to come here. She wondered how he'd managed
to get the time off so soon after his home leave.

She felt sick with fear. Oh, God, please, let everything
turn out all right. I love him. Don't let me ruin it now.

On and on she drove in silence, past Leesburg,
through winterish fields. The gently sloping hills dark
with evergreens were beautiful even at this time of year.
But the grass was colourless and the deciduous trees
were bare. Here and there a solitary farmhouse lay
sleepily in the quiet land.

Lunch was forgotten. Lauren didn't feel hungry
anyway; her stomach felt squeezed shut. Joel hadn't
moved for more than an hour and she kept just driving
on. The traffic was very light now that they'd left
Washington and environs and the road was good. Her
thoughts kept going around in circles and she wished
she could turn on the radio, but she was afraid to wake
Joel. She crossed the state line, entering West Virginia.
The wooded countryside was magnificent, would be a
true winter wonderland if covered by snow.

But it didn't snow. It rained. It poured. A deluge of
grey came down and blotted everything out. Lauren

could barely see, and she sighed with relief when she reached the town of Harper's Ferry. Having parked by the road, she shook Joel's shoulder. It seemed cruel to wake him up, but she had no choice. She had no idea where to go from here.

Joel opened his eyes and looked at her vacantly as if he wasn't registering who she was. Then he straightened and rubbed his neck. He groaned. Stiff muscles, no doubt.

'I'm sorry I had to wake you up, but I don't know where to go from here,' she said.

'Where are we?'

'It ain't Paradise,' she commented dryly, grimacing at the wet scene outside. 'Harper's Ferry, as you instructed.'

He raked his hand through his hair. 'Okay, let's find something to eat. I could use some coffee too.' He glanced at his watch. 'You made good time.'

'Good roads, good car. I like driving this machine. After being used to a Land Cruiser, this feels like a Rolls-Royce.'

'I know what you mean.' Joel peered outside. 'There's a diner not far from here. About one block, if I remember correctly. Just go slowly so we won't miss it. It's hard to see anything through this downpour.'

After sandwiches and coffee which they consumed in a somewhat strained atmosphere, they took off again, Joel driving this time. Lauren's hair was wet, her coat was wet, and her glasses were wet. Fortunately her feet were dry, stuck as they were in knee-high boots. She couldn't think of anything more uncomfortable than cold wet feet.

She dried her glasses with a handkerchief. 'How much farther is it?' she asked.

'Less than an hour. How long has it been raining like this?'

'It started about five minutes before I woke you up. I watched it coming. I was hoping it would be snow. This place would look like a picture postcard.'

'It isn't quite cold enough for snow, and it's just as well. I'm not sure we could have made it to the cabin. It's in the woods by a lake and the road is pretty treacherous in bad weather.'

'A cabin?' she queried.

'Yes.' He smiled wryly. 'I gave it away, didn't I? Well, it doesn't matter. We'll be there soon now.'

A cabin in the woods, alone with the man she loved—the stuff fantasies were made of. Romantic and idyllic. Except for one small detail: They weren't feeling very romantic. The air between them was not light and clear and clean, but heavy with suspicion and anger and fear.

It's my fault, she thought. Why did I have to over-react? Why couldn't I have . . . oh, what was the use? She felt wretched from the top of her head to the end of her toes.

'Is it your cabin?'

'No. It belongs to friends of mine in Washington. It's their weekend and summer hideaway. I called them last night and arranged to borrow it.'

'You called from Semarang?'

'Yes.'

'Why didn't you let me know you were coming?'

He shrugged. 'I didn't know until the last moment that I could actually make it. There were problems at work I wasn't supposed to be taking off in the first place. It seemed better to play it by ear. I suppose I could have called you from L.A., but I decided not to put you on the spot and see what happened when I found you.'

'I could have been in Nepal or Sri Lanka.' He would have made the whole trip for nothing.

Joel shook his head. 'I knew you'd be here. Don't ask me why, but I just knew.'

Strange thoughts, strange feelings. It had happened to her, this knowing without knowing. Was it merely instinct or intuition? She tried not to think about the bizarre things that had happened to her, but she couldn't help wondering what Joel would think if she told him about her vision, or remembrance, as Barbara sometimes called it. He wouldn't believe any of it.

She gazed at the rain still coming down in monumental quantities. They were winding around the hills on a narrow country road with the headlights on in the middle of the day. Lauren shivered involuntarily at the sight of the inhospitable terrain outside.

'Are you cold?' he asked. 'I can turn the heater up higher, if you like.'

'No, no, never mind. It's nothing. I hate this rain. Did the rains in Indonesia amount to anything this year? The day before I left we had the first real thunderstorm, remember that?'

He nodded. 'We've had a lot of those since. Mud baths everywhere. People flooded out of their houses in the *kampongs*. The drought is disastrous, the rains are disastrous. People can't win for losing.'

They fell silent again, which was just as well. The polite conversation was getting on her nerves. Her stomach was upset. Her head ached. She had the feeling she was supposed to do something, say something, but she didn't know what.

They arrived soon after that. The cabin was a rustic wooden affair overlooking the lake and surrounded by pine trees and overgrown junipers. A small jetty protruded into the lake, but there was no sign of a boat. It was probably in winter storage. Other cabins were visible here and there along the shore, but it seemed safe to assume that they were alone at this time of the year.

The key had been hidden under a rock somewhere and it took Joel a minute to locate it. Moments later they were inside, dripping water on a braided rug.

It was a lovely place. Having divested herself of her

wet coat, Lauren glanced around, shivering. She noticed the fireplace on the opposite wall. Paper, kindling and logs were already arranged, ready for a match. An old box was piled high with wood. There was comfortable, old-fashioned furniture, bright cushions and curtains, a few pretty prints on the plain wooden walls and shelves with paperbacks and magazines.

'What do you think?' His voice was even.

'It's lovely. . . cosy.' Romantic was really the right word.

Joel advanced into the room, picked up a note from the chunky wooden dining table and read it. There was a large bouquet of chrysanthemums on the table, a bowl of fruit, a big red candle, and a small cassette player with half a dozen tapes. Lauren picked them up and read the titles. Romantic music, every single one of them. Her heart contracted and she moved out of the room to look for the kitchen. It was small but convenient, with a big refrigerator with a freezer compartment, an electric stove, and wooden storage cabinets. The fridge was full of food—cheese, eggs, milk, liver pâté, condiments. The freezer was stocked with steaks and chicken legs and lamb chops and cans of frozen orange juice.

She opened the cabinets. Canned food of all kinds, and packages of rice and flour and spaghetti. On the counter, wrapped in a checked dish towel, lay a loaf of homemade bread. Obviously someone had been here not long ago and prepared everything for their visit. Except for perishables there was enough food for two or a couple of weeks.

Passing the living room, she noticed Joel on his haunches in front of the fireplace, lighting the paper with a match. He straightened, noticing her standing near the door.

'I'll get our cases from the car. I think the fire will just take off on its own. I'll be right back.' He strode out of the door and Lauren continued her exploration.

Another door led into a narrow hallway with thre
doors. There were two bedrooms and one bathroom
Only one of the bedrooms had been prepared.
fourposter bed, covered with a beautiful old patchwor
quilt, took up most of the room. A small table next t
the bed held a tray with a bottle of wine, two cryst
glasses and another candle.

There was movement behind her and she turned t
see Joel coming in with their luggage. His eyes swept th
room, then returned to her face. He gave her a crooke
little grin and lowered the suitcases to the floor.

'Mary is an incurable romantic, and that after te
years of marriage!'

Lauren tossed her hair back over her shoulders an
managed to return the smile. 'Yes.' She felt awkwar
She fingered the smooth wood of one of the bedposts.
had the deep sheen of age and care and felt satiny so
under her hands.

There certainly was no doubt that they were welcom
The place had been prepared for them with infinite ca
and obvious pleasure—prepared with love and romanc
in mind. And here she was with Joel in the most idyll
place she had ever seen and she was ready to crumble int
a thousand pieces from sheer nervousness and fear.

She stared at the quilt, at the hundreds of tiny piece
stitched together by hand into a beautiful pattern.
was a traditional design, but she couldn't remember th
name. She thought of the unknown woman who ha
spent all those countless hours piecing it together wit
endless patience.

'Come on,' said Joel evenly, 'let's make some tea o
coffee and sit in front of the fire and get warm.'

It was cold, and despite her wool skirt and sweate
Lauren shivered as she followed him to the kitchen. H
filled the kettle and put it on the stove. Openin
cabinets, he began to look for cups and spoons an
sugar. He located a can of Twining's Oolong tea.

'Ah, look at this,' he said. 'We have the real stuff here. Let's do this right. As long as we can skip the cucumber sandwiches—I never learned to appreciate them.'

'We have cookies.' Lauren opened an old-fashioned pottery cookie jar that stood on the counter. 'Look at this, homemade, no less. Oatmeal. You like them?'

'My favourite,' he said, grinning at her boyishly. He rinsed out the teapot with boiling water, spooned in the tea. 'Two for you and two for me, and one for the pot,' he counted.

'You really know how to do this right, don't you?'

'When I was twenty I had an English girl-friend. She threatened me. If I didn't learn to drink tea, she wouldn't marry me.'

'So you learned to drink tea.'

'Right. And didn't marry her.'

'What went wrong?' It seemed to be a safe enough subject, considering it had happened some fifteen years ago.

Joel looked at her gravely. 'I didn't learn to like the cucumber sandwiches.'

Lauren laughed. 'It couldn't have been true love, then. I've never heard of cucumber getting in the way of love!'

He poured water in the teapot and grinned. 'I told her my favourite sandwich was peanut butter with dill pickles.'

Lauren made a face. 'No wonder, then. It's revolting!'

'I didn't think so.'

She studied his face. 'You're kidding, aren't you?'

'No, I'm not. I was four years old when I first put pickles on my peanut butter sandwiches. I thought it was the culinary discovery of the century.'

'Yuk!' She put some cookies on a plate and arranged everything on a tray. 'If you take the pot, I'll carry this,' she said.

'Mary needs a trolley.' He looked around. 'And tea-cosy.'

There was none. He took a towel, folded it and put over the teapot. He consulted his watch. 'Five minutes

He was putting on this performance to lighten th atmosphere and ease the tension between them, Laure was well aware of that. They sat in front of the fire, th tea things between them on a low table, and we through the whole ceremony as if they were actors in play. When they were finished with their tea, she coul take the strain no longer.

'I'll see what I can do about dinner,' she said, puttin their empty cups back on the tray. She had a stron need to be alone, away from Joel.

'I'll help,' he offered.

'I can manage,' she said. 'The kitchen is really to small for two people, and besides, you're tired. Wh don't you just sit and relax for a while?' She picked u the tray and left the room, and to her relief Joel didn follow her.

There was a pan of beef stew in the refrigerator wit a note stuck on the lid. *It's Boeuf Bourguignon. All yo need to do is reheat it. Bon appetit!*

Reheating would take only a few minutes. It wasn enough time. They didn't need to eat for at leas another two hours. She needed something to do. salad—she could make a salad. Searching through th refrigerator, she assembled lettuce, tomatoes, onion and carrots, and put them on the counter. Washing an peeling and slicing would take some time. It was col Only the living room was warm because of the fir Well, she'd suffer through it.

She made the salad and washed the tea-cups. Whe she came back into the living room half an hour late Joel lay stretched out on the sofa, asleep. In a way sh was almost relieved. The fire needed more wood, an she took a couple of logs and carefully put them o

She zipped off her boots and stretched her legs towards
the fire. Oh, the warmth felt so nice! She picked up a
magazine from a nearby shelf and began to read.

Outside it was fully dark when she woke up. The fire
had made her drowsy and she'd drifted off to sleep. It
was still raining. They had turned on a lamp earlier and
the soft light spread out over Joel's sleeping form. He
hadn't moved a muscle. Total exhaustion—jet-lag.
He'd crossed twelve time zones, or was it eleven? His
night was day and his day was night, at least his body
thought so. No wonder he'd gone out like a light. She
could understand it, couldn't she?

Sure, sure.

Of course she wouldn't wake him up, probably
couldn't if she tried. It looked as if he'd be gone for a
while. His body needed to regenerate. Lauren got up,
found an afghan and covered him with it. She'd gone
through this herself; she knew all about it.

So why was she angry, upset, disappointed?

She put more wood on the fire and watched the
flames. She felt like shaking him. *You brought me here,
so don't you dare fall asleep on me!* she wanted to say.
*What am I going to do sitting here by myself? You
wanted me here, so do something!*

For a long time she just gazed at the flames, her
thoughts in turmoil. She tried to be realistic, but
couldn't. She'd never felt less romantic in her life, and it
was all his fault. She felt humiliated and resentful, and
the more she thought about it the angrier she became.
Some lover you are, Joel Rockwell!

Finally she went to the kitchen, buttered a slice of
bread and chewed it as she watched the rain coming
down. Then she made herself a cup of instant coffee
and carried it to the bedroom. There was a small
electric heater and she turned it on and sat at the edge
of the bed in front of it. Slowly she sipped the hot
coffee. She was going to take a long, hot shower. A

bath would be better, but there was no tub. Then sh
was going to take a sleeping pill and crawl under th
quilt and hope she wouldn't wake up until morning.

She had her doubts about that. She had no grea
confidence in the tablets that Barbara had brough
home one day. It was innocent, non-prescriptio
medicine Barbara had bought at the drugstore for her
but until now Lauren had refused to take any. Sh
didn't like medicine and even avoided taking aspirin i
at all possible.

Tonight she didn't want to lie awake. Her ablution
over and the sleeping pills ingested, she lay gazing up a
the bedroom ceiling, waiting for the miracle to happen
Her face felt very tight, as if it had solidified into ;
mask. She took a deep breath, rubbed her hands ove
her cheeks and tried to think peaceful thoughts. Sh
couldn't come up with any.

She should wake Joel and have a talk with him. No
better wait till tomorrow. Let him sleep.

Those damn pills aren't working! Why am I still lyin
here awake? I can't stand this!

This morning—it seemed years ago—she'd been on he
way to see her parents in Iowa. Somehow she'd ended u
in a cabin in some godforsaken wood in West Virginia
Alone in a fourposter bed. And the man she'd been achin
for lay asleep on the sofa, oblivious to her presence.

In the end the pills did work. Drowsiness sprea
through her body, warm now and cosy under the quil
and gratefully she let herself slip away into sleep.

This time it wasn't a dream.

She awoke to the sense of movement and touch
hands on her back, a face next to hers. A burnin
candle threw strange shadows across the wall. She wa
no longer alone in the fourposter bed. Under the quil
all was dark and secret and the hands caressing he
fanned her sleepy blood into fire. Only half consciou

she wrapped her arms around the warm, hard body, opening her mouth to the one covering hers with hungry intensity. From primitive depths came the sweet fever of love curling through her.

Arms and legs and mouths and hands moving, searching, stroking. Smooth skin. Hard muscles. Thick hair. His heart beating against hers, his breath mingling with hers. All was fluid, sensuous movement. She wanted to melt into him, meld their bodies.

A surging of life and joy and magic—on and on and on. He whispered to her wordless sounds and murmurs, stirring hidden memories of other times, of smouldering passion and singing senses. Then her name, over and over again. 'Lauren, Lauren, I want you so very much. . . .' Joel's voice, so strange and deep and rich, thrilling her senses. Inside her there was a silent answering. *I want you too. Love me . . . don't go away . . don't leave me. . . .*

Swimming back into her consciousness came other words, other thoughts. From deep inside her surfaced the fear and pain of other memories and a wave of chill reality washed over her. Oh, no! Not again, not only this. Oh, Joel, I couldn't bear it if you went away and left me . . . I couldn't! And the thoughts tumbled through her head, around and around until she felt dizzy with panic.

Floundering between swimming and sinking, she tried to push herself away, but his arms were too strong, holding on too tight. Her own body was fighting her, undermining her will and her reason. It wanted to drift back into that mindless feeling of warmth and wonder and sensuous delight.

'Lauren?' Bewilderment coloured his voice. His fingers touched her cheek, a gentle, caring gesture, and her throat ached.

'Let me go . . . please, Joel. I can't . . . I. . . .' She choked on the words and shut her eyes tightly to press back tears.

He lay still, his breath coming fast. Lauren opened her eyes, but his face was in shadow and she could not see his expression. She had to get away, from him, from herself, from that darkness between them. She struggled free, speech and thought frozen in her head, scrambled out of bed, picked up her robe from the chair and stumbled out of the room.

It was pitch dark and she bumped into a doorpost and then a table before finding the fireplace. Shivering, she huddled in front of it, seeing only a faint glow of ashes. Tightening the robe around her, she took in deep gulps of air. Her heart beat wildly against her ribs and she couldn't stop shaking.

So cold, so cold. . . . She rubbed her hands together. There was no feeling in them. Everything was cold—her fingers, her toes, her heart. No feeling. Cold. Frozen. She picked up some newspaper and crumpled it into balls. She threw them into the warm ashes, put some sticks and twigs on the paper and blew at it. The paper flared into flames. The kindling, too, began to burn. She arranged a couple of small logs in the fire and waited.

Minutes later all was dead again, except for some smoke curling up into the chimney. What had she done wrong? She had no experience building fires, but it had seemed easy enough. In California, in the summer, all you needed to do was drop a match and thousands of acres burned down. She couldn't even make a simple fire in a fireplace designed for the purpose. Reaching out, she dragged the afghan from the sofa and wrapped it around herself. She was going to freeze to death, and only minutes before she'd felt so warm, so safe. . . .

Tears were hot on her cheeks. Wiping at them, her fingers caught in her hair that hung in untidy tangles around her face. Oh, God, she was a mess! She couldn't even see clearly. Of course she couldn't. It was dark, she was crying, and her glasses were in the bedroom. She

ould turn a light on, at least. Her body refused to
move. Her muscles were stiff from the cold already.

What was the matter with her?

Why hadn't she wanted to make love?

Why was she acting so strangely?

Joel had come all the way from Java to see her. That
meant something. It *had* to mean something! Why was
he so terrified?

Suddenly a light came on and Joel, wearing jeans and
a bulky knit sweater, was next to her on the floor,
holding out a glass to her.

'Here, drink this. It's Scotch.'

Lauren gulped it down and the heat of it went down
her throat and into her stomach and spread all through
her body. Without a word, Joel set to work building the
fire and a short time later flames licked hungrily around
the logs. Why hadn't she been able to do that? Joel
turned and looked at her silently, then strode from the
room, returning a moment later with her glasses. He
handed them to her and she put them on.

'Thank you,' she said huskily. Why did her voice
sound so strange?

He answered with a little nod of his head. The silence
was nerve-wracking, a waiting hanging like an object in
the air between them. He poked around in the fire some
more and it came to a full blaze. Unmoving like a
stuffed toy, Lauren watched him. Was he angry with
her? She wondered if she should say she was sorry she'd
turned him down, that she hadn't meant to offend him.

Maybe he wasn't offended. She didn't know. She
couldn't tell anything from his expression or his
behaviour.

And suddenly she knew why she was afraid.
Suddenly she saw with clear lucidity what bothered
her, had always bothered her, about him.

He was too cool, too controlled. Except for those few
rare times he had spoken about Sharon, she had never

been able to tell what he felt or thought. She knew
nothing about his inner life, his feelings and emotions
She didn't know what he thought about her or what h
felt for her. It was all obscure and scary. She gazed a
his dark head and wondered how it was possible to lov
someone so much, knowing so little.

'Are you warm now?' he asked at last.

Lauren nodded. The fire was blazing and warming
her all through. Soon she would have to move becaus
she was sitting too close, but for now she wanted an
needed the heat.

The tension was almost palpable. She tried to think
of something to say, but her mind was a blank.

Joel raked his hand through his hair, giving her
bleak look. 'Lauren, I know I've done this all wrong
from the very beginning.' He paused for a moment a
if he didn't quite know how to go on. 'I intended to tall
to you as soon as we got here, explain myself to you
but instead I fell asleep like an octogenarian. I'm sorry

'You were tired. I know how it is. Didn't you have
stop-over in Honolulu or Los Angeles?'

His smile held no humour. 'No. I should have, o
course, but I didn't want to take the time. I was in to
much of a hurry to get here.'

There was a lump of pain in her throat.

He paced restlessly through the small room, stoppe
in front of the window and gazed outside. There wa
nothing but darkness and rain and cold. Lauren got u
from the floor and sat down in an overstuffed chai
hugging her knees. She watched his back. His shoulder
were slightly hunched. He seemed to be struggling wit
something and his cool, self-possessed air was no longe
evident. She wished she had the courage to go up t
him, take him in her arms and tell him she loved him
that nothing else mattered, as long as he loved he
too. . . .

She felt wretched. There was a knot in her stomach

turning and twisting. 'Joel,' she said, 'I'm glad you came for me. No matter what, I'm glad we're here.'

He turned slowly. His face was grey. 'Are you?'

'Yes.'

He looked away again, hands in his pockets. Hands that had held her only a short time ago. The feel of them was there on her body still.

The wind rattled the windows and the rain splashed down on the trees and the roof. The fire crackled and hissed. All those noises and still it seemed so quiet when they weren't talking.

'Lauren,' he began at last, 'I'm sorry I'm making everything so difficult for us. I've never been very good at handling my emotions.'

Lauren swallowed. 'Is anyone?' She certainly wasn't either.

'Some are better than others. All my life I've tried to . . . suppress . . . cover up my feelings. Partly because of culture, of course. Men are not supposed to show their emotions. And partly because of personal circumstances.' He turned and hesitated, looking at her for a moment. 'I became afraid of showing emotion. Even as a small boy I was good at hiding my feelings. It seems that I've always distrusted my emotions. I've let myself become dependent on reason. It seemed more reliable.' His eyes held hers for a moment. 'Do you understand what I mean?'

She nodded. 'Yes.' Oh, yes, she understood. How difficult it must be to live that way, how sad and unnecessary.

'Everywhere I look,' he went on, 'people get into trouble because of their emotions. They become irrational. They don't think things through. Sometimes they do the most dangerous things without even considering the consequences.'

Lauren straightened in her chair, tossing her hair back over her shoulders. 'And some of the most heroic things happen that way, too,' she said with quiet emphasis. 'People jump into freezing waters to save somebody from drowning. They run into burning buildings to rescue an old lady. I can't think of other examples, but you know what I mean. Emotion is what makes us *human*, Joel. We're not robots. We can't be practical and rational all the time.' She stopped abruptly. Why was she lecturing him?

'I know, I know,' he said impatiently. 'But there has to be some balance, a *natural* balance, and somehow I've never found it. I've fought my emotions all my life and my mind would always come out ahead. The safe way was always the one I could think through and analyse.' He sat down on the sofa, leaned his arms on his knees and stared at the floor.

The room was warm. It was almost three in the morning. No time to be out of bed, but here they were. After a while he raised his head and looked directly at her.

'I shouldn't have let you leave,' he said quietly. 'I wanted you to stay so badly, but my head kept interfering, telling me it was dumb, that it didn't make sense. Well, in the end I knew I'd made the wrong decision, and I'd made it with my head.' He looked away as if searching for words. It was silent for a while. 'My decision to marry Sharon was made with my head too, and it turned out to be wrong as well. It was the logical thing to do. All the pieces fit. I wanted to settle down. I was lonely and I wanted a family. Well, it was all there, ready made. It was all so comfortable and convenient. But something was missing and I didn't know it. I didn't *want* to know it. I ignored it. And then I met you.'

He hadn't looked at her while he was speaking. It was obvious how difficult it was for him to talk about this.

Lauren rested her chin on her knees and watched

him. Slumped shoulders, rumpled hair, lines in his face she hadn't seen before. His mouth looked pained and unhappy. Not the image of him she had carried with her everywhere—a picture of strength and intelligence and indestructibility. Was it an image only? A deity of her own mind's making? The real man was tired and uncertain and vulnerable like any other human being. No god, this, but a man with flaws and failures, battling loneliness and insecurities like the rest of mankind.

She loved him more now than she ever had.

She got up and sat down next to him on the couch.

He was looking down on his hands, clasping one with the other. 'Lauren, when I met you. . . .' He lowered his head in his hands and groaned. 'God, I don't know how to say this!'

Another silence. The silence of waiting—for revelation and understanding, for something that would make sense out of the feelings between them.

'Just say it,' she said, feeling hollow with helplessness.

He raised his head and scanned her face. 'When I first met you,' he repeated, 'I . . . something happened to me, something I'd never experienced before. I fell in love with you, instantly. The feeling was so overwhelming, it terrified me. There was no logic to it—I didn't even *know* you. Nothing like that had ever happened to me and I was horrified at the thought of losing my head, of doing something stupid, making a fool of myself. I tried to fight it. It was insanity to feel with such . . . *passion*. I felt I had to defend myself. And that's that I did. I had a damned *war* with myself! I went as far as leaving you to marry someone else. I tried to stay out of your way, but every time I went anywhere, there you were. It got worse and worse. It was like an obsession, and I thought I was going crazy.'

'You were very . . . very good at hiding it all. I. . . .' Her voice shook and she clamped her teeth together. All that had gone on in his mind and she hadn't known

it, had not understood what lay behind that cool,
composed exterior.

She knew a sudden flash of fury. Why? *Why?* All that
misery for no good reason. All those sleepless nights.
Oh, the waste of all those weeks! Senseless, *senseless!*
She'd had similar thoughts about incidents in other
people's lives: How could they let this happen? How
could they be so blind? Such waste, such unnecessary
pain. Now she was thinking the same things about
herself and Joel.

Her body felt rigid. She stared down at her hands
lying cramped together in her lap, knowing she wanted
to hit him, beat him, make him hurt like she'd hurt
inside for the last four months. She closed her eyes and
the urge passed.

'Are you angry?' he asked, putting his arm around
her.

Lauren shook her head numbly.

'Yes, you are,' he said quietly. 'I can feel it.'

'It's over now. I was angry only for a moment.'

Joel's arm tightened around her shoulder. 'Lauren,
will you look at me?'

She raised her face to him.

'When it comes to emotional things, I'm not very
good with words, Lauren.'

She didn't know what to say. Turning slightly, she
put her arms around his neck, her face against his. She
could feel the tension in his body. His mouth moved
across her cheek to her ear.

'I love you, Lauren,' he said unsteadily.

'I love you too,' she whispered. 'I loved you the first
time I saw you. I loved you all my life.'

'You're so good with words,' he murmured.

'Not very logical, though.'

'It doesn't matter. Love isn't logical, but I'll take it.'

She withdrew slightly and looked into his eyes. 'Will
you? No analysing? No questioning?'

'No analysing, no questioning. I tried it and it didn't do me any good. After you left I went through hell. I felt dead without you, and no amount of reasoning could get me out of it.' He smiled. 'I sound a bit dramatic, I know, but that's how I felt.' He drew her to him again as if he couldn't hold her close enough. His sweater felt warm and soft against her cheek. She thought of the wine and the candle and the fourposter bed.

He lifted her face and began to kiss her, and she closed her eyes. His hands slid under her robe and began to caress her bare skin.

'Lauren,' he said against her mouth, 'how do you feel about marriage?'

'It's a good way to be together,' she whispered back, feeling joy warming her like wine, making her feel light and carefree and sweetly dizzy.

Behind her closed eyelids she saw a beautiful room with red draperies and Oriental carpets, a courtyard with a sparkling fountain and a serene statue of the Virgin Mary. She thought about Joel, about the essence of love and the mysteries of the soul. She thought about logic and common sense, and about all those things for which there are no scientific explanations.

Another image flashed before her eyes—the laughing man riding away on his horse.

She opened her eyes and looked at Joel, solid and real and warm, with his arms securely around her.

Maybe, one day, she would tell him.

Coming Next Month in Harlequin Romance!

2653 DON'T CALL IT LOVE Lindsay Armstrong
He had fired four previous nannies for falling in love with the boss.
But he can't dismiss the newest applicant so easily. His little girl
needs her. And he *wants* her!

2654 THE FROZEN JUNGLE Jane Donnelly
A reporter receives an icy reception when she's marooned in the
Yorkshire Moors with the man she crossed a year ago. He's rough,
tough and dangerously sexy. And she's hoping for an early thaw.

2655 TWO DOZEN RED ROSES Rosemary Hammond
Roses are the last thing this secretary wants from her irresistible
boss. Roses from him mean the end of his latest love affair.
She knows...because she usually sends them.

2656 POLLY Betty Neels
A young woman of inner beauty falls in love with a handsome
professor who's used to gorgeous women with more sophistication.
She tries to run away from love. But her heart gives her away.

2657 ON SEPTEMBER HILL Leigh Michaels
Her sister's freedom carries an exorbitant price for a woman forced
to marry the man whose advances she once rejected with ease.

2658 A PLACE CALLED RAMBULARA Margaret Way
Can love prevail when an ordinary woman arouses the wrath of a
formidable temptress obsessed with desire for the most powerful
man in the Australian Outback? Yes — if it's strong enough.